MW01449808

You Are Not Here

Stories and Inspirations for Those Who Have Not Yet Arrived

Written by **Michael Albanese**

Illustrated by **JJ Richards**

Edited by **Chandi Lyn**

Copyright © The Weight of Ink, LLC 2024

First Edition - September 2024

All rights reserved.

ISBN 978-1-7328987-8-3

Created in The Town at Trilith, Fayetteville, Georgia

Handwritten inscription:

April,
You are a Blessing To All God puts in your path! Enjoy the stories from my favorite son-in-law! & Ns Him, Mr. ED (not the talking horse)

the
weight
of ink

I am not an adventurer by choice but by fate.
—Vincent Van Gogh

the
weight of ink

FOR WYNN

MY LOVE, PARTNER, AND MY CO-CAPTAIN.
YOU ARE MY WIND, MY SAILS, AND WHEN I NEED IT MOST, MY ANCHOR.
I CANNOT GET TO ITHAKA WITHOUT YOU.
I LOVE YOU SO MUCH.

FOREVER YOURS, MICHAEL

FOR ASHER AND GEORGIA

YOU BOTH ARE THE ABSOLUTE BEST PARTS OF YOUR MAMA AND ME.

I AM

SO GRATEFUL,

SO BLESSED,

SO AMAZED

I GET TO BE YOUR FATHER.

THE FUTURE IS BRIGHTER AND KINDER BECAUSE YOU BOTH EXIST.
I LOVE MY LADIES BEYOND WORDS!

I PRAY YOUR JOURNEYS WILL ALWAYS BE FILLED WITH ADVENTURES,
CREATIVITY, LOVE, GRACE. KINDNESS, AND GENEROSITY.

FOREVER YOURS, DADA.

Ithaka

Hope Your Road Is a Long One

You Are Not Alone	3
By Now	5
Why?	9
You Are Not Here	13

Don't Be Afraid of Them

Laestrygonians	15
Comparison	19
Expectations	21
No	25
Work	27
Health	31
Unsubscribe	33
Impostor Syndrome	37
Sobriety	43
Rejection	47
Emptiness	51
Content	55
Turbulence	59
Thirst	63

Many Summer Mornings

All Right On The Side Of Life	69
Failure	73
Marriage	76
Friendship	81
Enthusiasm	83
Better	85
Ideas	87
Dreams (A Poem)	89
Momentary Art	93
Reality	95

Inspiration	97
Perseverance	99
Kindness 9	101
Pho	103

Arriving There

Make It Medium	109
Maps and Compasses	113
Slowly Is The Fastest Way	115
The Envelope	119
I Still Haven't Found What I'm Looking For	121
Arriving	123
Enduring	125
Stamina	127
Half	129
They're Aggressive	133

Nothing Left To Give

Belonging	139
Fouls to Give	143
Forever Young	145
Terms and Conditions	149
Uncomfortable	151
Pull Up The Anchor	155
There Go I	159

Wise As You Will Have Become

Freshly Ground	165
Time	171
ROI	173
A Few Good People	175
Environment	177
Every Day You Get Older—That's the Law	181
Dulce Far Niente	183
Creative Resilience	187
The Marvelous Journey	193

Acknowledgements   *197*

ITHAKA

written by Constantine P. Cavafy, 1911

As you set out for Ithaka
hope your road is a long one,
full of adventure, full of discovery.
Laestrygonians, Cyclops, angry Poseidon—
don't be afraid of them:
you'll never find things like that on your way
as long as you keep your thoughts raised high,
as long as a rare excitement
stirs your spirit and your body.
Laestrygonians, Cyclops,
wild Poseidon—you won't encounter them
unless you bring them along inside your soul,
unless your soul sets them up in front of you.

Hope your road is a long one.
May there be **many summer mornings** when,
with what pleasure, what joy,
you enter harbors you're seeing for the first time;
may you stop at Phoenician trading stations
to buy fine things,
mother of pearl and coral, amber and ebony,
sensual perfume of every kind—
as many sensual perfumes as you can;
and may you visit many Egyptian cities
to learn and go on learning from their scholars.

Keep Ithaka always in your mind.
Arriving there is what you're destined for.
But don't hurry the journey at all.
Better if it lasts for years,
so you're old by the time you reach the island,
wealthy with all you've gained on the way,
not expecting Ithaka to make you rich.

Ithaka gave you the marvelous journey.
Without her, you wouldn't have set out.
She has **nothing left to give** you now.

And if you find her poor,
Ithaka won't have fooled you.
Wise as you will have become,
so full of experience,
you'll have understood by then
what these Ithakas mean.

HOPE YOUR ROAD IS A LONG ONE

*At this stage of your life . . .
are you where you thought you would be?*

YOU ARE NOT ALONE

While I would love you to believe that everything in this book is breathtakingly unique and boldly original . . . it is not.

There really is nothing new under the sun.

This book was partly inspired by *Ithaka*, a beloved poem written in 1911 by the Greek poet Constantine Cavafy.

Cavafy's poem was inspired by Homer's epic adventure, *The Odyssey*. Written almost three thousand years before Cavafy; *The Odyssey* is a perilous story of an embattled king's ten-year quest to return home to Ithaka and retake his throne.

C.S. Lewis once said, "Homer and Virgil wrote lines not for their own works alone but for the use of all their followers."

Old words become new again, to be seen with fresh eyes and interpreted by new minds, to resonate with new hearts, and to catalyze new work.

How many "heroes' journey" stories have been inspired by all that came before us?

For our purposes, Ithaka will represent our dreams and goals, the destinations we invest our time, energy, and passion in pursuing.

As with Odysseus, our journeys to Ithaka will not be linear. There are no direct roads, no shortcuts, and no such thing as a storm-less sea.

Our journeys will be defined by adversity and triumph.

Sometimes, our journey will take us to faraway places.

Other times, we can go far in life without having to go very far.

Everything in these pages reflects collected thoughts, ideas, and anecdotes (and maybe some clichés) from **my** journey, which has been, knowingly and unknowingly, inspired by many.

It skews toward a creative life as it is the only life I know.

I do not have any fancy degrees, nor did I attend college.

I will not pretend to be an expert in anything.

I may not have any business telling you how to live your life or pursue your dreams.

However, I do have my experiences, stories, perspective, and beliefs.

One of those beliefs is that we find books (or they find us) when we are most ready for them.

I hope this book finds you.

And I hope you find it encouraging.

There is no specific way to read *You Are Not Here*.

It is meant to be opened to any chapter in hopes that at any time, you will find something that provokes and inspires you anew, and reminds you that no matter where you are on *your* journey to Ithaka, **you are not alone.**

BY NOW

One bittersweet birthday, I was back in the town I most love.

My birthplace: New York City.

It is where my story began.

This concrete jungle was where I forged some of my closest friendships and discovered my love of the arts.

It is where my wife and I met, fell in love, and began our journey together—our origin story.

After eighteen years in Manhattan, ten years in Los Angeles, and half a decade in Atlanta, we finally took our daughters to New York City for the first time to help them understand their origin story.

Being there with my family on a milestone birthday was so sweet. However, it was bittersweet when I woke up that birthday morning and realized that I was **nowhere** near where I thought I would be at that age and stage of life.

The previous eighteen months were very challenging for several reasons.

Even though I was on the island of Manhattan, I thought, **by now,** I would have been on the island of Ithaka.

On this birthday, I felt overwhelmed. Yes, I was grateful to be alive and have another year of life. But I didn't know what my Ithaka was or if it existed.

I had lost my way. But I knew I was not alone. I started asking friends and colleagues in different circles and walks of life this question:

At this stage of your life,
are you where you thought you would be?

The majority responded, with honest fervor, "No."
"Why not?" I would ask. Some thought they would:
be married by now.
own a house by now.
have children by now.
have achieved more by now.
have had it all figured out by now.
have careers they wanted by now.
have conquered their addiction by now.
have overcome health challenges by now.
have a more significant impact on the world by now.
have moved out of their parent's house by now.
have a certain amount of money saved by now.
have/be (fill in the blank)

By now.

Two small, significant words.

But we are not on the island of **Ithaka** yet.

Better if it lasts for years,
So, you're old by the time you reach the island,
wealthy with all you've gained on the way,
not expecting Ithaka to make you rich.

There's the rub.

It is meant to be encouraging, illuminating the dark space between our dreams and realities.

It challenges our expectations, encouraging us to reach the island when we're old.

It also suggests arriving with no expectation of making you rich.

What? In *this* culture? How is that possible?

In the poem's final stanza, we discover two more small yet significant words:

By then.

***And if you find her poor, Ithaka won't have fooled you. Wise
as you will have become, so full of experience
You'll have understood by then what these Ithakas mean.***

*At this stage of your life,
are you where you thought you would be?*

Worry not, reader and friend.

You will become wealthy with all you have gained along the way. *

---

*This doesn't promise, imply, or guarantee financial or material wealth. It can, I suppose, but I believe it to mean something richer: the wealth of experience, wisdom, love, relationships, friendship, dreams, wonder, adversity, grace, joy, pain, and everything in between birth and death that tells our stories and maps the journey of our lives.

WHY?

Edward Albee was the first person I met in New York City. As a high school senior, I planned to move to Manhattan immediately after graduating. This involved selling a prized trumpet and selling my parents on the idea that I would attend a summer intensive at The American Academy of Dramatic Arts (six weeks in NYC that turned into eighteen years).

So, I did what any naive young man embarking on his creative journey to Ithaka would do.

I wrote a letter to Edward Albee.

Who would be better to show me the ropes than a Pulitzer-Prize-winning playwright?

Mr. Albee replied to my letter with a postcard from Europe and an invitation to call him when I arrived in New York City.

So, I did.

I met him at his Tribeca loft during my first week in New York. That afternoon, we spent five hours drinking coffee and eating oatmeal cookies.

That was the beginning of a mercurial, finite friendship.

I was too young then to appreciate what I know now, that he was a genius, and whether you love all of his work or not, he was one of the greatest American playwrights.

Albee was a challenging mentor. Fiercely honest, his presence was unnerving. Every conversation was cryptically fascinating yet riddled with tension, which felt dangerous.

Reading and watching his plays (and many others) taught me that the truth **is** dangerous.

In those early years, when I was trying to figure out what I was meant to do, he gave me gifts in the form of truth.

He was the first person to suggest (insist, really) that I was not a very good actor (I learned that truth myself over time.)

But he was also the first to encourage me to write a play.

So, I did.

It forever connected me to something I deeply love.

I credit him with my discovery of writing, my love for theater, and all the art forms through which stories are told.

Edward Albee once told me:

"I write to figure out *why* I am writing."

Likewise, I am writing this book to figure out **why** I am writing this book.

Les impers mastics, Paris, 1977 © John Batho 1985

Dear Michael — Thanks for your note & photos. I'll be back from Europe the end of June & will be happy to meet with you in N.Y.C. in July. (I don't know that I have anything specific for you then....) Call me at 212- when you get in.
Regards, Edward Albee

Michael V. Albanese
Marietta,
Georgia.
30064

YOU ARE NOT HERE

YOU ARE NOT HERE

Do you remember shopping malls?

Before Covid. And the Internet. When we could drive ourselves to what was *then* the coolest place to hang out with friends.

Inside the mall was a large map on each floor with a diagram of the retailers and restaurants.

On the map was an X followed by the words:

YOU ARE HERE

It is reassuring to know where you are.

But for me, I was directionally challenged, so this map was never helpful. I never knew where *here* was, so I would wander around the mall until I arrived at my destination.

Now I wonder:

What if we were standing in front of a map of our life?

Our maps would look different, as each life journey is unique, but they are all used similarly: to navigate and symbolize.

What would *your* map look like?

Mine would chart my life's zigzagged routes and accidental (or divine) pinpoints. It would include all the missteps, misdirection, and mistakes and likely reveal the uncertain, circuitous course I have taken to get to . . . today.

For some of us who thought we would have arrived by now, we may see a big X in the middle of our life map with the words:

YOU ARE *NOT* HERE

What do you mean?

What happened?

I thought I would be there by now.

Well, the map says otherwise.

The route was confusing.

The directions were unclear.

The compass broke.

We got lost along the way.

We ran out of gas.

Our engine quit.

The boat sank.

We go from wanderlust to wondering:

Will we ever get there? Does it even matter now?

Under the big X on the map of your life there is sometimes the stinging reminder that you are not where you thought you would be.

But if you look closely, there are encouraging words that are often hard to see (believe) . . .

. . . you are exactly where you are supposed to be.

DON'T BE AFRAID OF THEM

LAESTRYGONIANS

According to mythology, the Laestrygonians in Cavafy's poem are man-eating giants from Sicily.

Well, my family originates from Sicily. But we are Laestrygonians only in the kitchen—pasta-eating giants.

Of course, these man-eating giants are just mythological.

In the real world, on our actual journeys, we confront far more significant threats. The list of dream-eating, energy-sucking, time-wasting ogres is myriad.

Here are some I thought of:

Addiction	Bullying	Rejection
Hopelessness	Cruelty	Hate
Loneliness	Discouragement	Division
Self-sabotage	Comparison	Racism
Unkindness	Despair	Narcissism
Lying	Depression	Corruption
Stealing	Confusion	Deception
Cheating	Toxic People	Dejection
War	Toxic Places	What else can **you** add?
Mass Shootings	Expectations	

Sometimes, they consume us, making us stop, frozen in fear. However, we can move past these giants when we rebel against them by keeping our thoughts raised high.

We can keep moving forward, even when we have been pushed back.

Do not be afraid. Do not be afraid of them.

All noble things are difficult
—Oswald Chambers

COMPARISON

Comparison is the thief of joy.

—Theodore Roosevelt

My daughter and I are reading a book for school called "Bully for You, Teddy Roosevelt," which has introduced me to fascinating facts about the 26th President of the United States I didn't know (or forgot.

Roosevelt's quote about comparison resonates.

Plenty of research exposes comparison for what it is—deadly to wellbeing.

Comparing your life to others leads to increased feelings of depression, stress, and anxiety coupled with decreased creativity and motivation. This generates the perfect storm, undoing and undermining the precious steps we take on our journey.

Social media has accelerated the comparisons and made their outcomes even more deadly.

The World Health Organization estimates close to one million suicides worldwide each year, making it the second leading cause of death among people fifteen to thirty years old.

If you look too hard at those who have more than you, you will never be able to see what you have.

World Health Organization. (2023, August 28. Suicide. www.who.int/news-room/fact-sheets/detail/suicide

If you look too hard at those who have more than you, you will never be able to see what you have.

And those who have less will be forgotten.

It's not about how much you have—or don't have.

Always and forever, there will be those with more and many more with less. None of that matters.

There is only *one* **you** on this planet.

Unique, purposed, and beautiful.

You are the only you in your home, school, workplace, community, or place of worship.

Be grateful to have this special place in the world during this fascinating time in our history.

Don't compare and despair. It will steal your joy.

This seems like such a cliche now, but . . . be **you.**

EXPECTATIONS

Expectation is the root of all heartache.

– William Shakespeare

I cannot list all of the times I've had an aching heart from the expectations I put on others and myself.

Some of the most profound pains I have experienced creatively, relationally, spiritually, and financially have been rooted in expectations.

Unhealthy and unrealistic expectations can lead to all kinds of modern grief.

Perfectionism, codependency, failure to draw personal boundaries, unrealistic self-image, entitlement, delusion, narcissism, stubbornness, ego, apathy, atrophy, the need for immediate gratification, savior complexes, etc.

However, to guide the ship back on course, we can pursue healthier expectations of ourselves.

We won't always get it right.

Often, the expectations we put on ourselves are the most impossible.

But with some grace and deliberate practice, we can aim to expect ourselves to be kind, just, fair, honest, loving, mindful, generous, merciful, interested, servant leaders, stewards of our gifts and responsibilities, seekers of truth and knowledge, and respectful.

Blessed is he who expects nothing,
for he shall never be disappointed.
— Alexander Pope

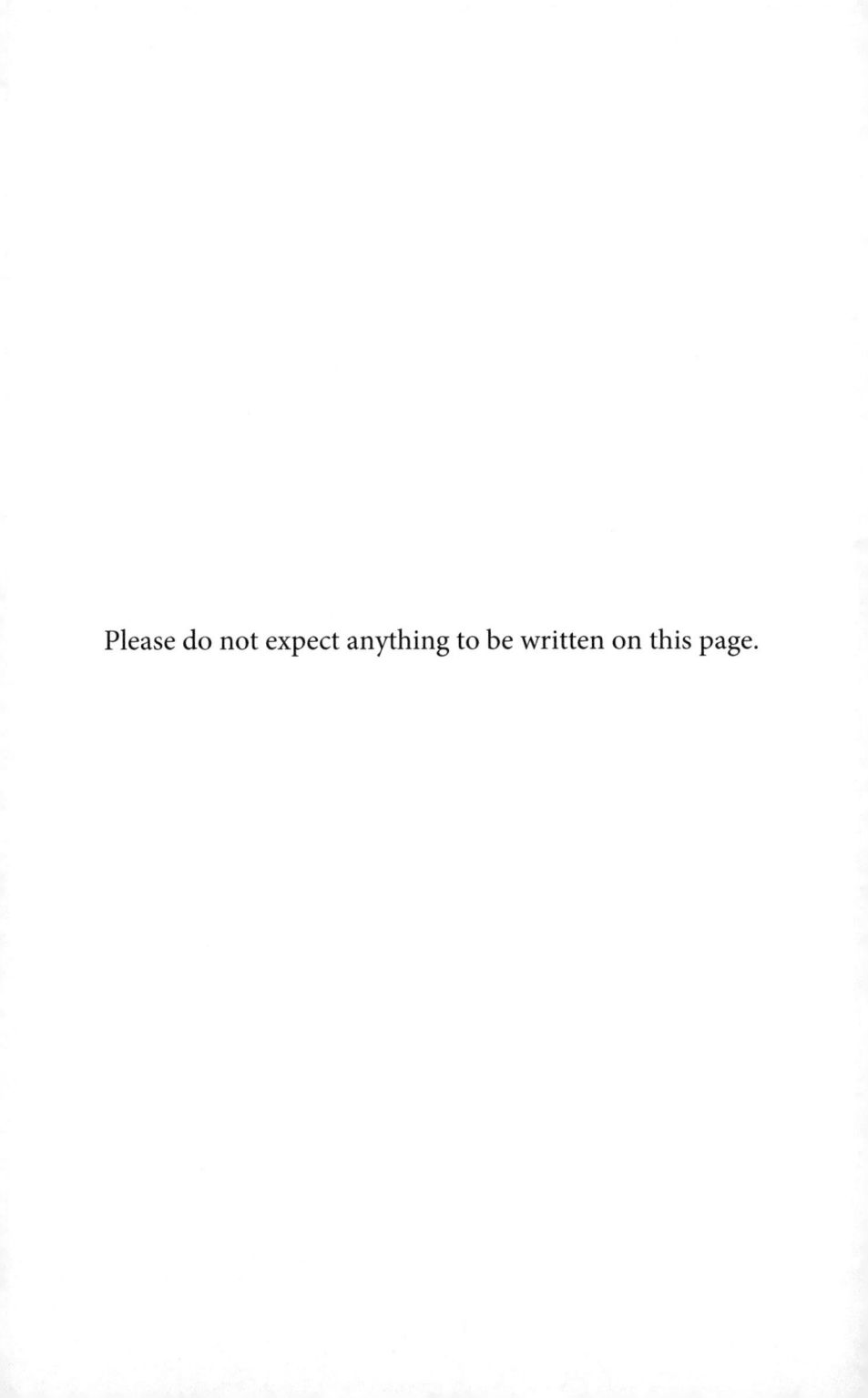

Please do not expect anything to be written on this page.

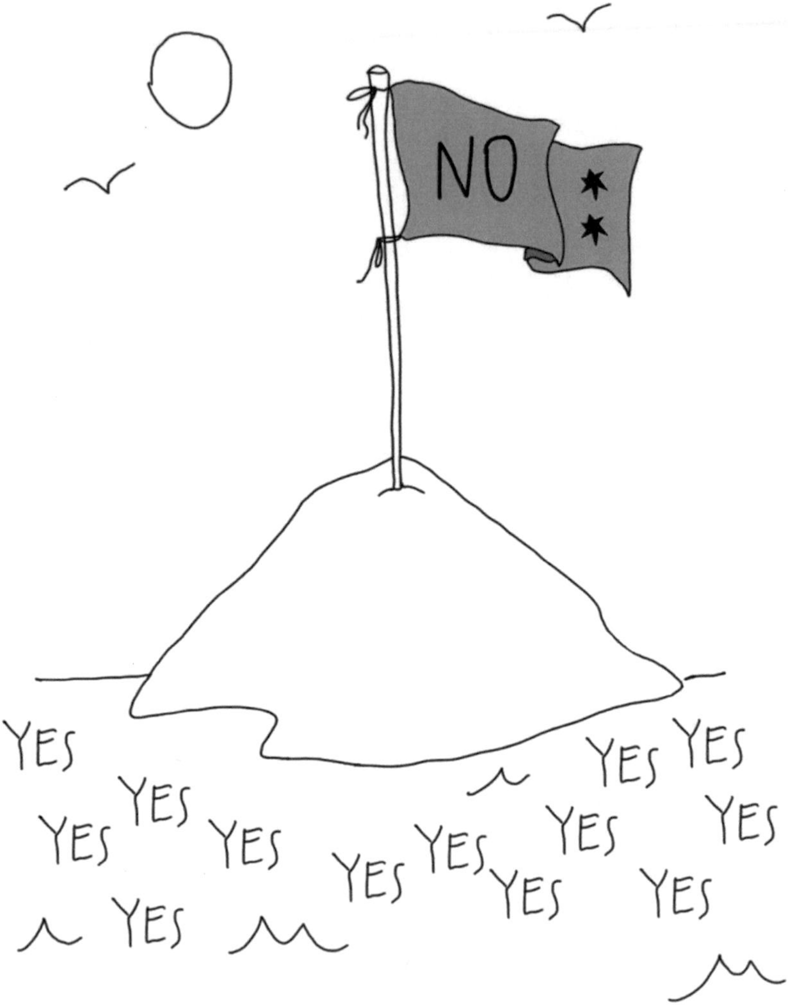
NO
YES
YES
YES
YES
YES
YES
YES
YES
YES
YES
YES
YES
YES
YES

NO

The answer "no" is better than *no* answer.

I coined this phrase years ago when I would submit my work to publishers, production companies, agents, or producers—and then never hear *anything*. But here is the reality:

People are busy. And—nobody owes you or me anything.

Nobody is obligated to read, like, or get our work.

But I am old-school regarding common courtesies, even if they come as rejection.

We seem to think the word *no* is always negative.

It appears like a rejection, but what if it is a hidden opportunity to re-prioritize your time, energy, and goals?

What if saying no is saying yes?

In his book *Principles,* Ray Dalio states:

> *You have to say no to things you want*
> *so you can say yes to things you want more.*

So, it is not just saying no to the things we know we should say no to (toxic and destructive habits, mindsets, behaviors, and people) but having the courage to say no to **good** things—to the things we want—so we can say yes to the things in life we want **more**.

Think about how many opportunities we have each day to say no to the competing interests vying for our time, energy, and hearts.

Your nos can be in service to your yeses.

Write down five things you want in life.

Write down five things you want even more.

What is the alchemy in your life that will make this conversion possible?

WORK

I don't like work. No man does.
But I like what is in the work— the chance to find yourself.
— Joseph Campbell

I have worked many jobs throughout my life, compass tight in hand, following a messy map that has led me to where I am now. Here is a list of some of the jobs I have worked. A lot of them, *I did not like*, but I did like the chance to find myself.

- Lawn Mower
- Grocery Bagger
- Burger Flipper
- Skin Care Salesman
- Car Valet
- Legal Courier
- Appliance Repairman
- GAP Employee
- Dishwasher
- Waiter
- Caterer
- Food Expeditor
- Bus Boy
- Bartender*
- Restaurant Manager
- Barista
- Envelope Stuffer
- Temp Worker
- Kosher BBQ Manager
- Nightclub Worker
- Legal Assistant
- Executive Assistant
- Personal Assistant
- Production Assistant
- Director's Assistant
- Health Club Receptionist
- Assistant Director
- Tea Salon Manager
- Line Producer
- Producer
- Actor
- Concierge
- Consultant
- Entrepreneur
- Landlord
- Publisher
- Writer
- Whatever is next...

*see "Thirst"

Most of these I treated as *survival jobs*.

Little did I know at the time, but they were **arrival jobs**, each helping me arrive at the next opportunity, the next experience, the next challenge, the next collaboration, the next skill to endure the next mile of the journey.

If you are currently doing work you do *not* want to do as you work toward the work you *do* want to do, consider it a gift.

You will arrive more skilled, experienced, and well-rounded.

You don't have to like your job.

But can you like what is in your job — *the chance to find yourself?*

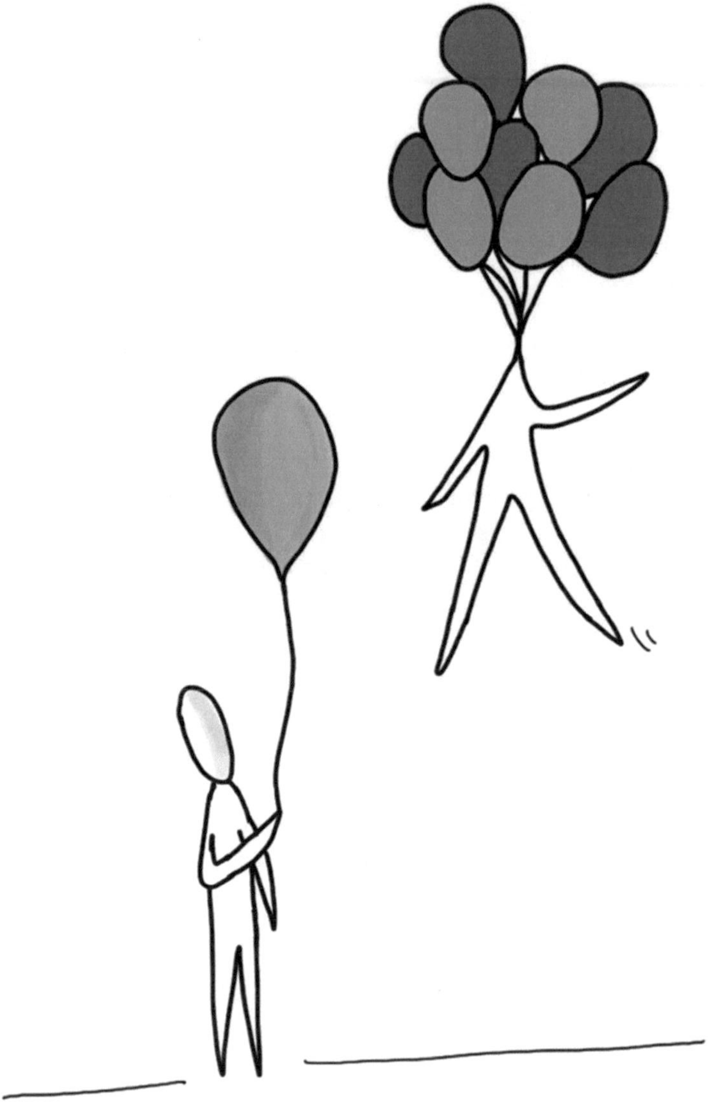

HEALTH

A healthy person has a hundred dreams.
*A sick person only has **one**.*

My wife is the best mother and life partner I know. She is also very talented and works full time as an actor.

Her work is both a blessing and a source of anxiety because in 2012, a deadly bacterial infection in her gut altered her life suddenly and forever.

She has had a recurrent infection three times.

She almost had her colon removed.

She almost died.

She battles an invisible enemy daily.

Even today as I write this, she received news she will need another procedure, the same one that initially set this health crisis in motion.

If good health is a line of dominoes, this procedure was the incident that pushed the first domino into a chain reaction.

Like most challenges, we never saw it coming.

For twelve years, we have been searching for the magical elixir (our pantry filled with hundreds of supplements offers plenty of evidence).

We have consulted with over a hundred doctors, allopathic and naturopathic, and have had countless Zoom, phone, and email consultations with providers around the world, from New York to Nashville to South Africa.

We were even once scammed out of $500 by an alleged naturopathic doctor in Mexico.

It is a roller coaster of despair and hope.

And the search continues.

Our faith has been challenged, refined, and redefined.

But my wife's resilience is stunning.

She is a mother, works full-time as an actor, nurtures friendships, and continues cultivating her artistry.

We never expected this when we embarked on our journey together. Who does?

But it is still rich and challenging, and we are still hopeful.

Health is wealth.

You don't know what you've got until it's gone.

(I told you there would be some cliches).

Anyone who has suffered a health crisis and/or loved somebody who has knows this to be true.

Yet.

It is possible to fully live between the tension of trial and hope, challenge and blessing.

We live in that complex, beautiful tension right now.

UNSUBSCRIBE

If only I had a dollar for every time I unsubscribed to something.

I unsubscribe from at least 3 to 5 emails per day and purchased software that helps allocate marketing emails to a separate folder so they don't clog up my inbox.

Everyone is selling something. Including me.

When this book is complete, I will sell it.

But it is not just marketing emails or small-press books vying for our precious time, attention, and money.

Our culture, politics, family, media, and friends want us to subscribe to something.

These things are not wrong or ill-intentioned, and you may enjoy subscribing to any or all of them.

But we must be careful with our resources, time being the most important and non-renewable.

Unsubscribe from anything or anyone that:

turns your no into a yes

converts production into distraction

is toxic

does not align with your values

impairs the ability to hear what we need to hear does not

align with your goals, dreams, and intentions

IMPOSTOR SYNDROME

When I was a kid, I fell in love with magic and illusion.

I loved the thrill of learning and performing a trick.

I loved showmanship and being able to pull off something that left friends and family scratching their heads in disbelief.

(I am giving myself too much credit; I wasn't that good.)

But I think what I loved most was becoming somebody I wasn't (which eventually made sense when I discovered acting—see "Belonging").

I was comfortable being an impostor.

In my junior year of high school, the then President of the United States, George H.W. Bush, was running for re-election. It was announced that he would stop in my hometown for a rally, and he would rally at my high school gymnasium.

The city was electrified, and so was the high school band. The band director had us immediately start rehearsing "Hail to the Chief," the patriotic anthem to welcome the leader of the free world. Trumpet in hand, I practiced my heart out.

A week before the President's arrival, the Secret Service swept our high school as part of its protocol. They walked the hallways of our school and the gymnasium, where their boss would eventually speak. They had cool suits, dark sunglasses, and killer dogs. *I was enamored*.

I woke up extra early on a cold Saturday morning in February. I showered, put an abnormal amount of gel in my hair, slicked it back, and slipped into a black suit and tie.

I found an old earpiece plugged into the television, stuck it inside my ear, and then wrapped the cord around it and into an inside jacket pocket. I slipped on a pair of black Ray-Ban sunglasses (the most significant purchase I had ever made. I borrowed one of my father's thin black Samsonite briefcases. I was ready for action. I could not be more prepared to be the ultimate impostor— a Secret Service Agent.

But wait. I was missing something to give that extra flair.

Handcuffs. I had a trick pair of handcuffs in my magic kit, so I handcuffed my wrist to the briefcase and walked out the door. To be clear, the handcuffs were not standard Secret Service protocol.

I parked a few blocks away from the high school. After all, my cover would have been blown if somebody saw me pull up in a faded yellow 1972 Delta 88 Oldsmobile.

I walked swiftly toward my school, breathing in rhythm with each determined stride. Turning the corner, I saw hundreds of people waiting patiently outside the gymnasium.

I put my shoulders back, picked up my pace, and walked directly toward the crowd. Something remarkable happened.

They parted like the Red Sea.

I continued walking toward the entrance of the gym and up the stairs. This was the moment.

I walked past the *real* Secret Service and into the gym, where only the press and Secret Service were allowed.

Success.

With bravado, I walked down the bleachers to the basketball floor. There, waiting for me, was a platform stage with a podium.

This is where the President of the United States would soon speak, so it made perfect sense to position myself on the stage, a few feet behind the podium.

Reminder: I still have my sunglasses on, my earpiece in, and a top-secret briefcase containing top-secret documents handcuffed to my top-secret wrist. I played the part beautifully.

Soon after that, the band assembled in a semi-circle.

My childhood best friends, Willie and Raymond, were fellow trumpeters and warmed up with the band. However, there was a mysteriously empty seat in the trumpet section.

Secret Service was positioned around the gymnasium and at all entrances, one of which was directly behind me, the back door to the gym.

The front doors opened, and the general public shuffled in, filling the bleachers.

The energy was palpable. I was excited and nervous but remained still and stoic, trying not to draw any attention to myself. I had to stay in character, a challenge, as I saw my family enter and walk down the bleachers looking for seating. They, of course, were looking toward the band to see their son (and big brother doing something special and unique.

Upon realizing I was not where I was supposed to be, my father started looking around; his calm demeanor belied an otherwise panic-stricken parent. He looked on the platform stage, and there I was—his Secret Service son—with *his* briefcase handcuffed to my wrist. He turned ghost-white and sat down, trying not to make a scene.

I slowly lowered my sunglasses, locked eyes with my father, and gave him a wink. I don't know what made me do it; I just hoped he'd be impressed with my accomplishment.

The gym was packed. Suddenly, the door behind me opened. The band was queued.

♪ *Hail to the Chief we have chosen for the nation, Hail to the Chief, and we salute him one and all!* ♪

The President marched in the back door with his cavalcade, approaching the stage and behind the podium.

The crowd went wild. The noise was deafening. The band was playing. My chest was pulsating.

The most powerful man in the world was standing a few feet away from me.

I do not remember a single word President Bush said, how long he spoke, or what he spoke about. The whole moment was so surreal that the next thing I knew, he finished his speech and exited as quickly as he entered the gymnasium. But this time, I followed along with the cavalcade. After all, I was the high-ranking Briefcase Man.

(By the way, I recently learned that a briefcase man goes everywhere with the President carrying the nuclear war buttons. It is called "the football" because, in the original atomic war plan, this was called "dropkick.")

I exited the gymnasium. The Presidential motorcade went one way, I the other, back to my Oldsmobile Delta 88.

I removed the earpiece. I felt like I was walking on air.

I went directly to a Waffle House, still in my suit, tie, and sunglasses. I enjoyed a Presidential breakfast: a waffle, hash browns smothered and covered, and weak Waffle House coffee.

It was a pivotal moment in my life. I pulled something off that no other sixteen-year-old had ever done. Consequently, I was kicked out of the band, nearly kicked out of the house, and my father almost had a heart attack.

The following year, I moved to New York City.

I share this story because I went from loving being the impostor to hating my impostor syndrome as I grew older.

If most of us are honest, we have experienced this psychological phenomenon of seeing ourselves as a fake or fraud, and it's just a matter of time before the world finds out.

During the 2020 Covid pandemic, my impostor syndrome was heightened. Having work and income replaced with fear and anxiety caused me to doubt my accomplishments and success. I felt unqualified to own a business and had a cartoonish perspective on my ideas and writing.

I was paranoid, always thinking that somebody would call me out and say, "You're just not that good, are you?"

Yet, there have been periods of my life when I have experienced the Dunning-Kruger Effect—which is the opposite of impostor syndrome. This is when your lack of skills in a particular area causes you to overestimate your confidence and competency—the "fake it until you make it" model.

We often live in the tension between overconfidence and under-confidence.

But the goal is to live in **authentic** confidence—a confidence that blossoms from being who you are meant to be instead of pretending to be somebody else. Oscar Wilde once said, "Be yourself; everyone else is already taken."

Authentic confidence is born in the humble acceptance that we are still working in progress, constantly learning and evolving with an innate desire to grow into whom we were created to become, whether that is an aspiring member of a marching band, a world-class magician, or . . . an actual Secret Service Agent.

SOBRIETY

I grew up with a grandfather and two uncles who died from alcoholism. Many of my friends and colleagues suffered from substance use disorders. Some still do.

I have a friend named Jason who, thankfully, this past January 2024, celebrated seven years of sobriety after a long, difficult battle with addiction.

I encouraged him to turn the "one-minute reads" he posted on Facebook about his journey from addiction to recovery into a book I eventually helped publish.

My friend Daniel was kind enough to design the cover based on his artistic interpretation of the material.

Another friend, Anthony, was generous enough to help produce a book launch event. These men are also in recovery and share an ordinary yet amazing grace.

Being in that space for a year with Jason and reading his work engaged my reticular activation system. It seemed that everywhere I went, I met somebody in recovery willing to share their journey from addiction hell to the freedom of sobriety.

Their lives and speech were imbued with humility, urgency, and vitality. These were men and women who stared their demons in the face and lived to talk about the grace and restoration that came from sobriety. Their capacity for hope, gratitude, and love was palpable.

They did not need to impersonate or pretend to be somebody they were not.

They no longer need to have all the answers.

They no longer needed to be perfect, to perform or create an illusionary version of themselves.

Some fantastic gentlemen collect the trash in my neighborhood. They are graduates of a beloved local recovery program called A Better Way.

When you converse with these guys, they are singing, smiling, and filled with joy.

This was undeniably due to their faith in a God of their *own* understanding.

They are fellow journeymen with their own Ithakas, despairs, and dreams.

I encourage anyone to sit down for a coffee and ask them to tell you their story.

You will find a refreshing honesty and vulnerability not often found among those still held in the grip of addiction.

To learn more about Jason and his story, please visit:
jasonumidi.com

To learn more about A Better Way Ministries, please visit:
abetterwayministries.com

REJECTION

Rejection is to the artistic process as storm clouds are to a beautiful day. It is a natural part of a creative atmosphere.

On dark, stormy days, it is good to remember that the sun of enthusiasm will shine again. However, while that sun is shining, it is also a healthy reminder that not everyone will:

> ... *get* **your work.**
>
> ... *want* **your work.**
>
> ... *understand* **your work.**
>
> ... *embrace* **your work.**
>
> ... *pay you for* **your work.**

That's okay. That's a good thing.

You can't be all things to all people.

And neither can your work.

I have a collection of rejection letters and emails that could fill The Library of Congress.

Getting rejected from anything, especially something you create, can be unpleasant.

But I have come to believe that:

Rejection is protection.

As painful as rejection is, it could be protecting you from something—or someone—even more painful.

Sometimes, what we think gives hope instead hands us despair.

You might be rejected from a/an ...

>					opportunity
>
>					job
>
>					promotion
>
>					date
>
>					assignment
>
>					team
>
>					position
>
>					board
>
>					grant
>
>					fellowship
>
>					university
>
>					school
>
>					role
>
>					competition
>
>					residency
>
>					loan
>
>					contest
>
>					exhibition
>
>					scholarship
>
>					publishing submission
>
> ... but there is a chance you are being divinely protected from something you cannot see.

*"We must see our work as divine in origin.
We must believe there is a divine path of goodness
ahead in its unfolding.
When we are rejected, we must ask,
What next and not – why me?"*

—Julia Cameron, Finding Water

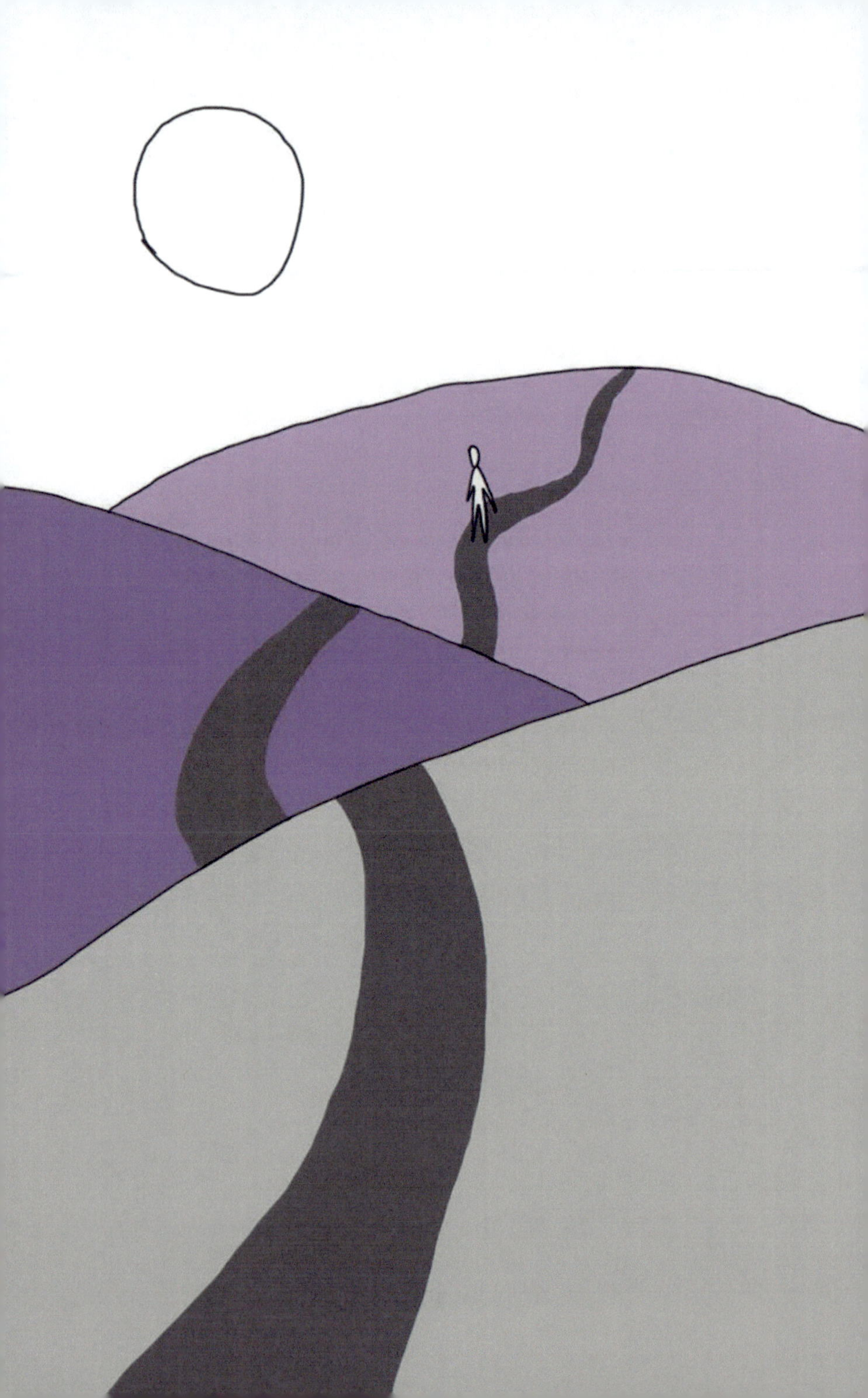

EMPTINESS

Just today, I received an email from a client whom I would also consider a friend. He is a successful venture capitalist, having invested in over 100 companies throughout his career. He is Ivy League-educated, creative, and professionally accomplished. On paper, he has it all.

He is having an existential crisis. He considers his recent efforts to build a new company and run for public office both failures. He does not know what is next in his life and career.

He has not arrived.

Take athletes who achieved immense success.

Rob Gronkowski, the All-Pro tight end who helped lead the New England Patriots to four Super Bowl championships, often felt like he was losing, even after he won. "…if we won a game, the next day, it felt like we still lost," Gronkowski said. "And if we lost a game, it felt like you were in super-depression for like two days … or like for the whole week."

One of my favorite actors, Daniel Day-Lewis, has won three Academy Awards, but in 2017, he quit acting because of his crippling depression. Nicole Kidman won an Academy Award for her portrayal of Virginia Woolf in *The Hours*. In a 2013 interview with Harper's Bazaar, she said, "Winning an Oscar made me realize how empty my life was."

Paracelsus Recovery is a clinic that has treated many celebrities for addiction and depression. According to the Swiss-based recovery center's research, Academy Award winners are seven times more likely to suffer from mental health addiction than other people.

Dr. Paul Hokemeyer, the psychotherapist and author of *Fragile Power: Why Having Everything is Never Enough*, claims celebrities have a fragile sense of power that can break at any point.

"Fame should come with a health warning," says English singer Robbie Williams.

I am not a celebrity or venture capitalist. I have not won a Super Bowl or an Academy Award, but I sank a game-winning 3-pointer in a basketball game the other night. That evening, as I lay in bed, I felt empty. I could only think about the shots I missed.

Whether it is winning the most significant title in American football, the biggest honor for the craft of acting, or exiting a successful venture capital firm, the emptiness seems to mock our most signifigant achievements.

How can we feel empty after victory? How do we fill the space that was supposed to overflow with . . . fulfillment?

When I sink into the quicksand of self-focus, here are three ways I crawl out (not always successfully:

1. I focus on and connect with others.
2. I take a pencil to paper and write out everything I am thankful for.
3. I pray and seek deeper intimacy in my Christian faith, which sometimes precedes and enhances #1 and #2

I also turn to wiser minds, like Cavafy and his poem:

> Keep Ithaka always in your mind.
> Arriving there is what you're destined for.

Then, later in the poem:

> Ithaka gave you the marvelous journey.
> Without her you would not have set out.
> She has nothing left to give you now.

As I struggled through this, I discovered something called *arrival fallacy*: the false assumption that once you achieve something, happiness will follow. Coined by Tal Ben-Shahar, who holds a PhD in Organizational Behavior from Harvard, the arrival fallacy is an illusion that happiness is discovered in achievement.

Reality reveals this truth in sports, business, the arts, and life.

The poem suggests that Ithaka (our goal, destination, achievement, or arrival gives us the journey and that without her, we would not have set out (tried, ambitioned, dreamed, etc.)

The reward **is** the marvelous journey we have been given.

"Joy (fulfillment) can only be real if people look upon their life as a service and have a definite object in life outside themselves and their personal happiness."
—Leo Tolstoy

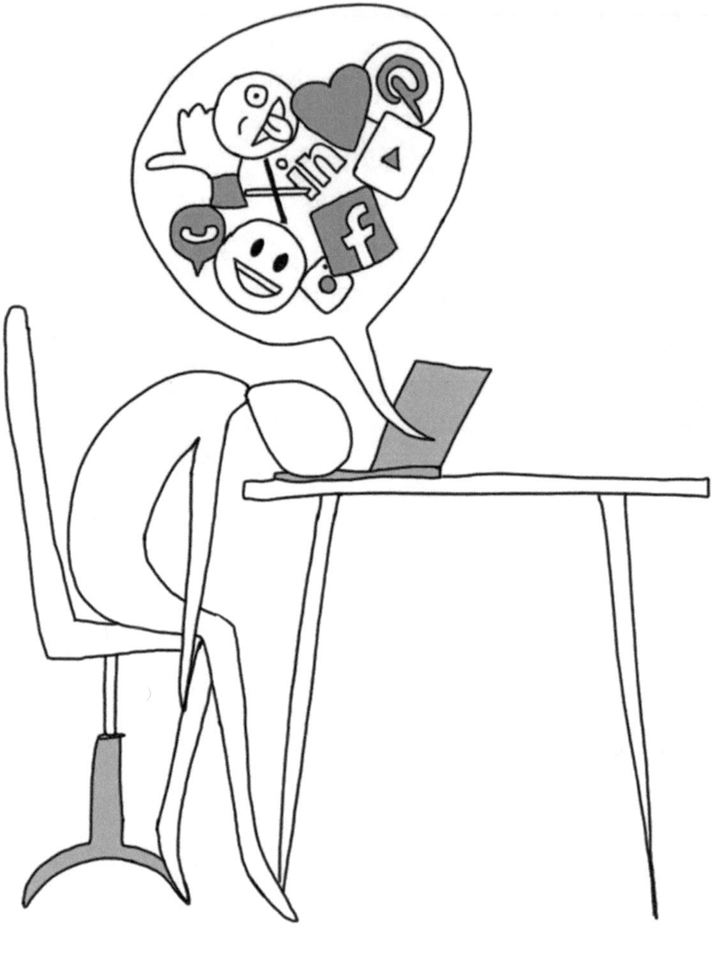

CONTENT

As the transformational trends of technology continue to evolve rapidly, so does a market's insatiable demand for content.

Everyone, it seems, creates "content."

But is some of this content (um, politics?) making our culture . . . contentious?

There are hundreds of streaming channels, millions of podcasts, and hundreds of millions of blogs worldwide. Human beings cannot possibly consume all the content created by human beings, and this does not even consider the amount of content AI will create.

90% of the world's data was created in the last two years alone.

Every minute, users upload 500 hours of video to YouTube.

Over 2.5 quintillion bytes of data are created each day.

When the pandemic shut down the world, humanity's creative spirit soared by creating some of the most inspirational, beautiful, and educational content we have ever seen.

Not to mention entertaining.

Photography, magic, cooking, comedy, parenting, sourdough bread making, storytelling, literature, motivation, fitness, wellness, basketball, politics, investing, gardening, travel, and adventure, etc.

The list of stunning content is endlessly mind-blowing.

Unfortunately, the amount of asinine, low-brow, pointless, and fake content is equally mind-blowing.

But back to the good stuff with a plug for my sister, Allison. She built a beautiful platform featuring content she created from her extensive worldwide travels and culinary experiences. Inspired by an intellectual curiosity and deep passion to share her discoveries with the world, she creates content daily at parchedaroundtheworld.com

We are overwhelmed with content.

But are we . . . **content?**

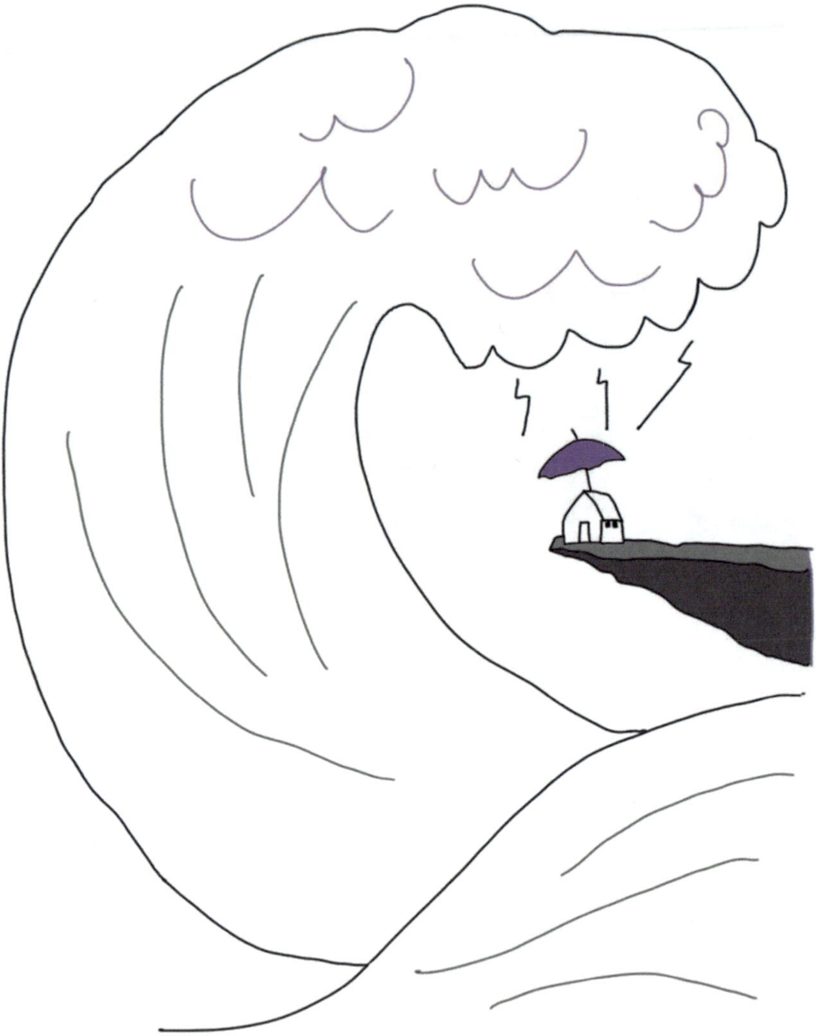

TURBULENCE

I hate turbulence. I don't know anyone who *loves* it. Except maybe for children, pilots, and sadomasochists.

My childhood friend, Shervin, an excellent pilot and surgeon, assures me there is nothing to worry about.

What I have noticed about turbulence, especially as the plane climbs to the desired altitude, is that you often encounter a cloudy environment where everything is obscured. You cannot see anything above or below you. The plane is literally in the clouds.

It is disorienting.

But as you continue climbing through the shakes and bumps, you eventually rise above unstable air until the sky becomes brighter and clearer, with everything once again visible—and, for me, relieving.

This does not surprise or bother the pilots flying these miracles of aviation. They are trained to encounter all kinds of turbulence and can accurately forecast and avoid the conditions that cause it.

If we are the pilots of our lives, how do we deal with the turbulence of life?

We do not train in a simulator. We train in the air, in real-time, in an authentic atmosphere, with real pressure and turbulent conditions. Our training is extensive and ongoing.

We learn to take off, climb, fight through unexpected rough air, and sometimes make emergency landings.

And if we're honest, sometimes we crash.

From my experience, some people are most comfortable with turbulence (e.g., drama, negativity, toxicity, corruption).

They prefer a cloudy, murky atmosphere. They are not interested in helping you with your oxygen mask.

They don't want to climb to higher ways of being.

They would rather keep you in the middle seat next to them, flying indefinitely through unstable air without visibility.

But the rare others keep climbing.

They are prepared for rough air.

They've been there before.

They know what bumps feel like, and they continue fighting through unpredictable directions in airflow and intense pressure until that first ray of sunlight bursts brightly above the clouds.

This is rarefied air.

This is the atmosphere where you live, free of dark clouds and miserable instability. Here, the visibility is clear.

But don't get too comfortable.

There is clear air turbulence in life, too—the things we didn't see coming, the wave of uncertainty, the unexpected that didn't appear on our radar.

This could be a pandemic, a diagnosis, a breakup, or a breakdown.

Good pilots always expect the unexpected and course correct.

Do not be afraid of turbulence.

It is natural and often provides the lift we need to rise above the clouds and start seeing our lives more clearly.

**When you come out of the storm,
you won't be the same person who walked in.
That's what this storm is all about.**

—Haruki Murakami

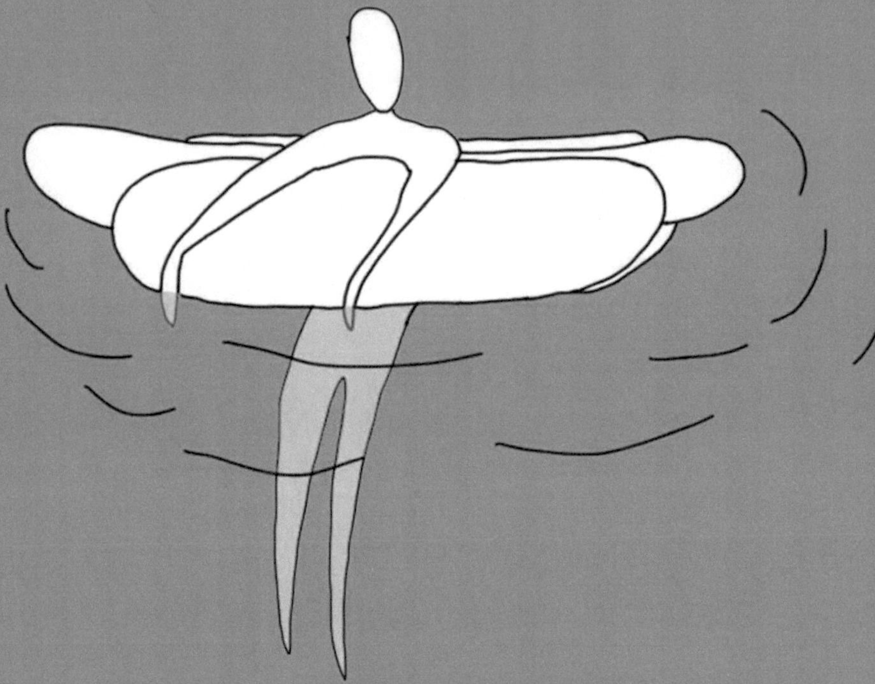

THIRST

I was once almost homeless in New York City.

I was living in Hell's Kitchen when it was . . . hellacious.

In between jobs, I could barely make ends meet.

I had no money saved. Nothing stashed away for a rainy day, nor any cash hidden in a futon or coffee can.
I rifled through dresser drawers and pen cups, searching for loose change, anything I could cobble together to pay for coffee or a sandwich.

It was a dark time in my life.

I was in this dark place due to the circumstances I created for myself through a series of imprudent decisions.

(I think the Latin phrase for imprudent is **dumb ass.**)

I left my apartment on West 46th Street and proceeded to walk along 9th Avenue, seeking work.

Diners, laundromats, restaurants, pet shops, and hardware stores—whatever it was, I didn't care. I went everywhere asking for work and was repeatedly denied.

It was disheartening until I walked into this one bar.

I approached the bartender and, as humbly as I could, asked for a job.

"I'll do anything," I said.

With pity in his eyes, the bartender asked me to take a seat at the bar and wait. He disappeared for a few minutes before returning with a plain hot dog, which he graciously handed to me.

It was the best hot dog I had ever eaten.

I still remember the taste.

I will never forget this simple act of mercy.

The bartender explained that there was nothing at the bar for me to do. However, their sister bar—located in the bowels of Port Authority Bus Station—needed someone to work the next three nights because their bartender had appendicitis and required immediate surgery.

After I finished my hot dog, he instructed me to go to the bar nine blocks south, and ask for Teddy. I promptly ran down to the bar and found him, a tall, emaciated man behind the bar. He was holding his side and sweating.

He had seen better days. And so had I.

Teddy handed me the keys to the bar, grunted, "Good luck," and hobbled out.

That was it.

I gazed around in dismay. The bar was small and dark, and a haze of stale cigarette smoke hovered like storm clouds. Denizens were at the bar, their faces wrought with despair.

This was not a "fun" bar.

This was not where you came for Instagram-worthy cocktails after work with a colleague.

This was the last stop for the last call.

This was where people came to drink themselves to death.

I tucked the keys in my pocket and reluctantly walked behind the bar, greeted with grunts and groans from the regulars.

It was 5:00 p.m., and I was told the bar closed at 4:00 a.m. It was going to be a long night, serving hard liquor to hard faces in plastic cups for $2.50 a drink.

Suddenly, my unfortunate life situation did not seem quite so . . . unfortunate.

As the night went on, the barstools filled with patrons.

They drank and smoked and drank and smoked some more. This went on all night and until the early morning. Crumpled dollar bills tumbled across the bar in exchange for the next drink. I'd slide back two quarters in change, and they would wave it off or tell me to keep it. My tip jar was filled with quarters.

At 4:00 a.m., I ushered the customers off their stools and out of the bar. I locked the door behind them as they stumbled into a dark morning. Where they went, I had no idea. But they were back twelve hours later, lined up outside at 4:00pm, waiting for the new kid with the keys.

We did it all again for the next two nights. After the final night, I went home and took the hottest shower I could tolerate.

Then I sat on the linoleum floor of my Hell's Kitchen apartment and counted my tips.

I made $450 that weekend. It was a fortune.

It was a reminder that **"but for the grace of God, there go I..."** (see the chapter "There go I" for more context.

I will never forget that weekend.

I will never forget how a hot dog and a bartender helped me survive another day by providing food and opportunity.

I'll never be able to thank Teddy for having appendicitis and for giving me the chance to earn money and gain perspective.

For years, the memory haunted me.

I eventually wrote about the experience and produced a film called *Thirst*, directed by Rachel McDonald and starring Melanie Griffith, Josh Pence, and Gale Harold.

Sometimes, our most challenging circumstances are hidden gifts that unwrap themselves over time.

MANY SUMMER MORNINGS

ALL RIGHT ON THE SIDE OF LIFE

ALL RIGHT ON THE SIDE OF LIFE

I learned I was a rule breaker in the first grade when I got on the wrong bus. To me, it was the *right* bus. I was supposed to board the bus that would take me to Kinder Kare, where my parents would later collect me after they returned from work. But one day of after-school care was all I needed to know:

I was going to things my way.

One afternoon, I sneaked onto the regular school bus that dropped me off at Greenbriar Parkway, a small road that meandered into the woods. There were only two houses on Greenbriar Parkway, mine and our neighbors, separated by a broken-down, red wooden fence.

I got off the bus at the corner, walked right through my front door, directly to the refrigerator, and promptly consumed an entire container of Cool Whip. I then called my mother at work and told her I was home alone but safe.

Oddly, and thankfully, she was fine with it.

Our backyard was exactly an acre, flanked by a bank on the right lined with sunflowers and a forest to the left.

Nobody was around except my only neighbor, who was never home (I later learned he worked for the CIA.

That day set a precedent.

It was the first time I experienced freedom.

When I was six years old, I would come home from school, make a snack, and embark on grand adventures. I wandered through the woods, waded in the creek, rolled down the embankment, and spent blissful hours alone, lost in the gift of childhood imagination.

It is where I created my first known personal mantra:

ALL RIGHT ON THE SIDE OF LIFE!

I am unsure what this meant, but I would repeat it out loud with romantic enthusiasm. It seems silly now, but to the six-year-old me, this was a proclamation, a philosophy, a kaleidoscope of hope through which I viewed the world.

This was before my siblings, before that entire land got deforested and turned into a large, residential neighborhood, and before it would be considered insane to allow a first grader to spend hours unattended after school.

If my children did that now, I would lose my mind.

But then, it was just paradise. It was my Eden.

I often reflect on the purity of that childhood innocence. Yet, it's been a long time since I declared "all right on the side of life."

For some of us, getting to Ithaka means first returning to innocence. We desire to end up where we started.

Others never knew the innocence of childhood to begin with, and life now is a pursuit to heal from trauma and discover it for the first time.

Our journeys are messy, uncertain, and sometimes just really difficult, if not hopeless.

Progress, industrialism, technology, the political divide, expansion, human nature, culture, and the relentless pursuit of "self" have separated us from our paradises.

If the journey is the reward and the destination is simply a place to gratefully lay out the gifts we have gathered along the way, I am hopeful that when we arrive, we can say, in our own ways:

All Right on the Side of Life

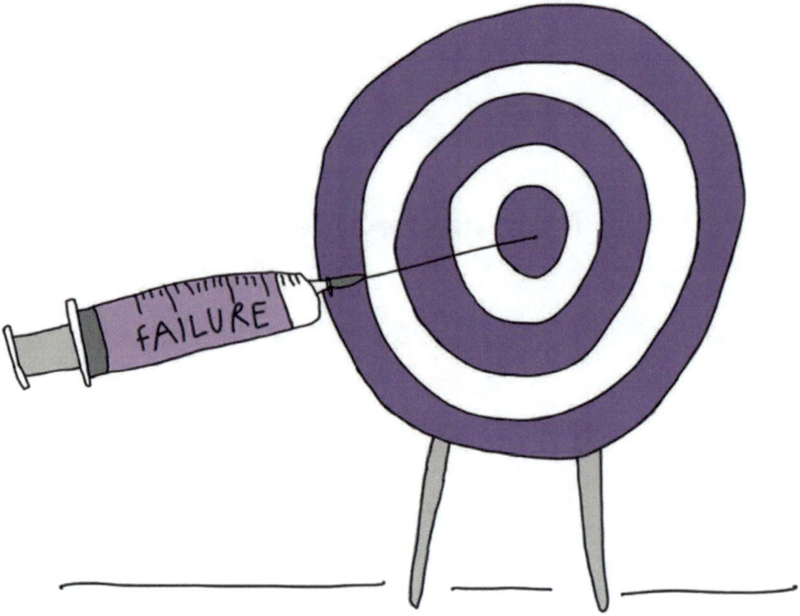
FAILURE

FAILURE

In recent years, there has been a vicious debate around vaccinations.

(I won't dare discuss that here.)

Vaccines are made of the things they are supposed to create an immunity against. They contain ingredients meant to trigger an immune response against itself. The polio virus contains poliomyelitis or polio. The Measles, Mumps, and Rubella vaccines contain a weaker version of the virus it is meant to fight. For our purposes, we will explore the "F word"—failure.

Failure is a vaccine against failure.

The more you fail, the stronger your immune system against failure becomes.

You cannot receive this vaccine unless you:

Try
Risk
Work
Serve
Dream
Imagine
Try again
Stay humble
Keep working
Are vulnerable
Enjoy the process
And then try again
Put yourself out there
Release perfectionism
Keep trying again and again

However, this is a vaccine nobody can force you to take.

I am inoculated.

I have failed so many times that I am now immune to it.

In 2020, I created a card game inspired by the popular childhood game "Old Maid." Since it was politically themed, I released it in time for the Presidential election.

There was something for everyone.

I created a Democrat Deck with Donald Trump as the "old maid" in drag and a Republican Deck with Joe Biden as the "old maid" with pigtails (it is mid-2024 now and *here we go again*).

I had never created a card game before. I had no idea how to do it. I just figured it out.

I had zero fear of failing. And I thought it would sell out overnight.

But the truth is—it failed.

I did not recoup the money, time, and energy invested in creating the game. It took a year to produce the final deck, art-directing each card, develop cost-effective printing and shipping, build an e-commerce website, and release and market a political game in perhaps one of the most caustically divisive elections in recent history.

The other truth is—that it succeeded.

It succeeded because an idea was extracted from the ether and executed into something you can hold in your hands and play.

The feedback was great, if not amusing.
Customers loved the game.
Our friends, Russ and Kara, take the game on their travels and send photos of their family playing it everywhere from Mexico to Greece.

This does not make the project profitable, but it does make it rewarding. I no longer make decisions based on the fear of failure. I make them based on the inevitability of success.

As Rick Rubin says, "Failure is the information you need to get to where you are going."

Because I have redefined success for myself, I always succeed. But not in the ways you may think. I don't always succeed financially. I don't always succeed critically. Some of the closest people in my life have not "gotten" my work. Some of my books (this one likely will be no exception have been slammed by readers.

We succeed by finishing, completing, executing, sharing, and doing it all over again.

"Don't be a hoarder," admonishes Austin Kleon in his inspiring little book, *Show Your Work*.

That does not mean every idea we have must be completed, executed, and shared. I have also learned that the hard way (see the upcoming chapter: "Idea Cemetery").

But on your way to Ithaka, you must define—and redefine — success for *yourself*.

If you do not, success will be defined *for* you.

Become a successful failure.

If you want to purchase your very own Presidential Old Maid deck and help me get rid of this inventory in time for another crazy Presidential Election, please visit the QR code below and use discount code YANH for 50% off.

Silence is not just the absence of sound
but the presence of grace.
—Madeline L'Engle

MARRIAGE

Madeline L'Engle is one of my favorite authors.

A Wrinkle in Time and *Walking on Water* are some of her best fiction and non-fiction works, respectively.

Her marriage to actor Hugh Franklin has always inspired my wife and me. We have always wished to emulate their creative, spiritual, and honest relationship, even though we never knew or met them.

I remember us, newly married, sitting in a coffee shop in New York City many years ago and stumbling across something L'Engle wrote about her marriage.

We are the protector of one another's silence.

How beautiful and intimate; we can be so woven together that we can protect one another's silence.

We have honored this idea for two decades and recently celebrated our twentieth wedding anniversary.

When we need silence, sometimes a subtle nod is sufficient to engage this vital practice.

We need times of silence.

To retreat from one another, even from our partners.

And it doesn't have to be a physical retreat.

There is something powerful about being together in silence.

There is something powerful about being alone in silence.

When I was a child and we went to the movies, before the film began, there was always an animated advertisement promoting: "Silence is Golden."

This life we lead is noisy and sometimes exhaustingly complex. The world's messaging constantly attacks, often times misaligns and pierces our needed silence.

As with life, marriage can be a messy, uncertain process. Protecting each other in moments of silence is critical.

The growth of love is not a straight line.

L'Engle said in *Two Part Invention*, her engaging book about marriage:

> *Marriage is not just spiritual communion.*
> *You have to remember to take out the trash.*

Speaking of which,
somewhere in my house,
a litter box needs cleaning.

A bonus thought about silence:

Michaela Coel was the first African-American woman to win the Emmy Award for Outstanding Writing for a Limited Series, Movie, or Dramatic Special at the 73rd Primetime Emmy Awards.

This is part of her acceptance speech:

"In a world that entices us to browse through the lives of others to help us better determine how we feel about ourselves, and to, in turn, feel the need to be constantly visible, for visibility these days seems to somehow equate to success. Do not be afraid to disappear from it, from us, for a while and see what comes to you in the silence."

What could come to **you** in the silence?

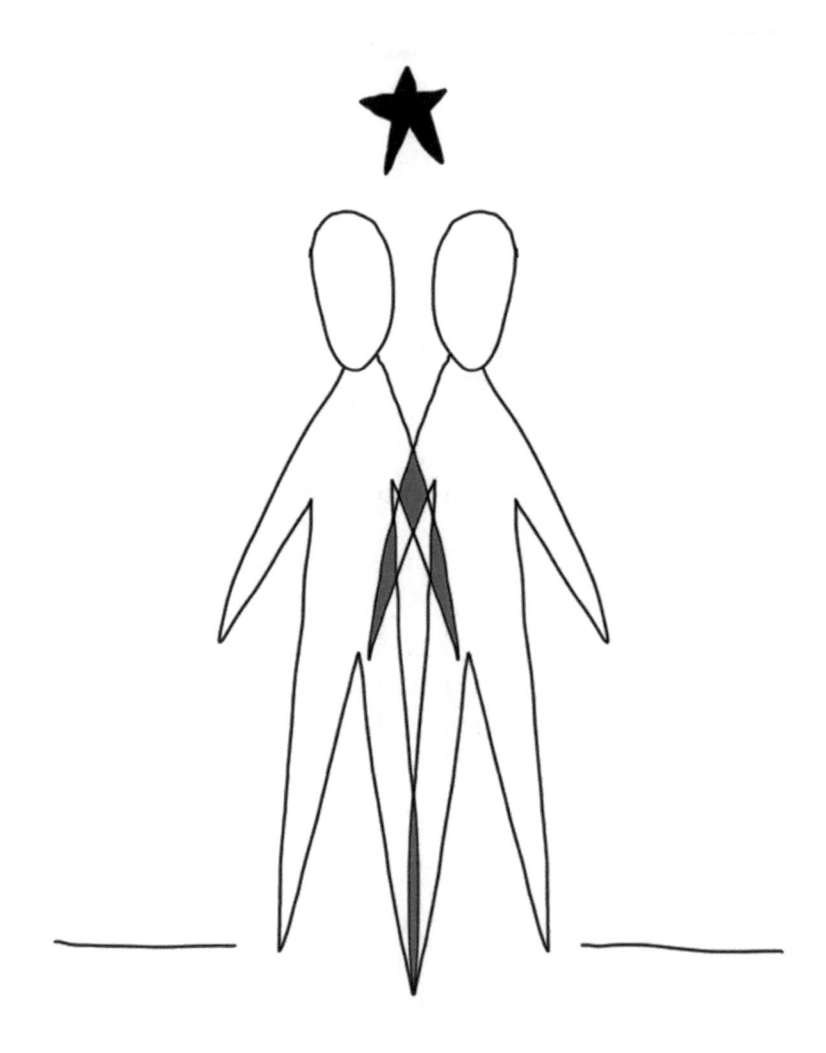

FRIENDSHIP

Park Slope, Brooklyn: I was having coffee with one of my roommates and closest friends, Nick Cokas, who at the time was a successful Broadway actor.

We shared a vulnerable moment of melancholy, discussing how the weight of the world was bearing down on us. We were both going through tough seasons for several reasons.

Nick turned to me and said, "We see life in slow motion."

That always stuck with me.

Sometimes, we stay busy to avoid the slow, deliberate motions of sitting in pain, discomfort, and change.

When you see life in slow motion, you see reality for what it was always meant to be—real.

We do not journey nor arrive to Ithaka alone.

We were created to be in relationships, and one of the most powerful relationships on our journey is the gift of friendship.

I am fortunate to have such long-standing, loyal, and iron-sharpening-iron friendships.

Some of my closest friends today are those I met in third grade, junior high, and high school.

My adult friendships were forged in the early days of living in New York City and in later years in Los Angeles.

I am developing and rekindling new friendships in Georgia.

Friendships are eventually tested, shaped, and strengthened by the joys and trials of life.

I am in the season of life where the parents of friends are passing away.

Recently, I attended the funeral of one of my best friend's fathers.

There will be another season in the future when I attend the funerals of my friends. And they will attend mine.

Today is a beautiful day to reach out and say hello.

Your friends won't be here forever.

And neither will you.

ENTHUSIASM

***As long as a rare excitement
stirs your spirit and your body.***

Ralph Waldo Emerson once said "Nothing great was ever achieved without enthusiasm."

As a poet and philosopher, Emerson believed enthusiasm was a vital force that inspired personal growth, creativity, and a more meaningful connection to each other.

When was the last time you were enthusiastic?

What were the circumstances? Who were you with?

What nourishes your enthusiasm?

I am drawn to the dreamers and risk-takers.

And I know it requires tremendous excitement and passion to keep dreaming and risking.

We often struggle to maintain enthusiasm, especially amid setbacks and failures.

One of my my favorite and encouraging quotes is from Abraham Lincoln:

Success consists of going from failure to failure without loss of enthusiasm.

What can you do today to re-ignite your enthusiasm?

What can you do to encourage enthusiasm in others?

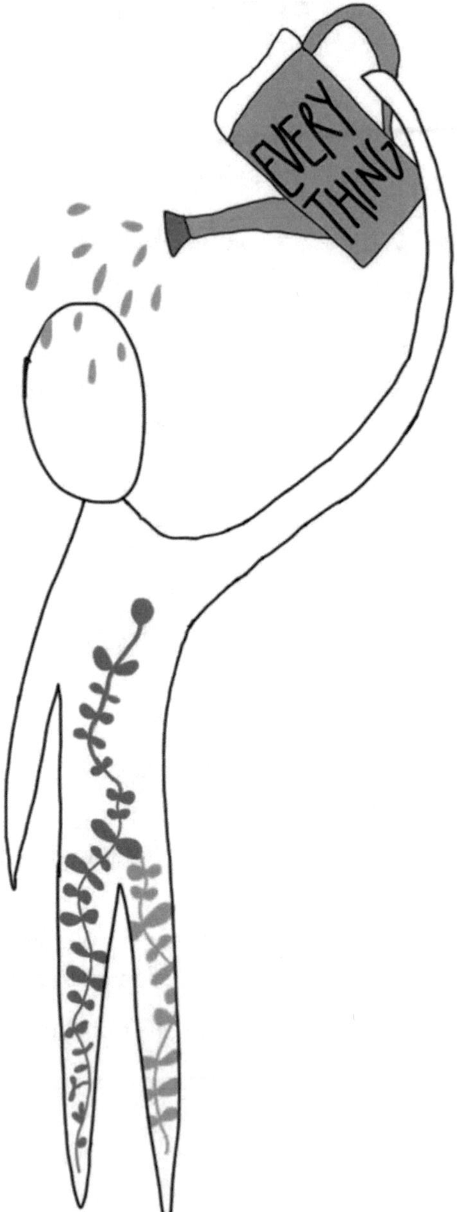
EVERY THING

BETTER

Our dear friend Craig Archibald is a lovely, kind human being.

He is an actor, writer, and a wonderful acting coach.

Craig coaches with intention and purpose.

There is no guru-ism here, just practical truths on navigating the mindset, business, and life as an actor.

He admonishes his students and friends alike to *make everything make them better.*

We often do not have a choice in what happens to us, but we can choose how we respond.

Will these things make us bitter?

Or will they make us **better**?

To make everything make us better is not easy.

It requires discipline, resilience, and courage.

If we learn to make everything make us better, we will build the necessary fortitude for the next leg of the journey.

What is bitter in your life that you can use to make you better?

If you are interested in Craig Archibald's encouraging and enlightening book, *The Actor's Mindset*, you can find it on Amazon.

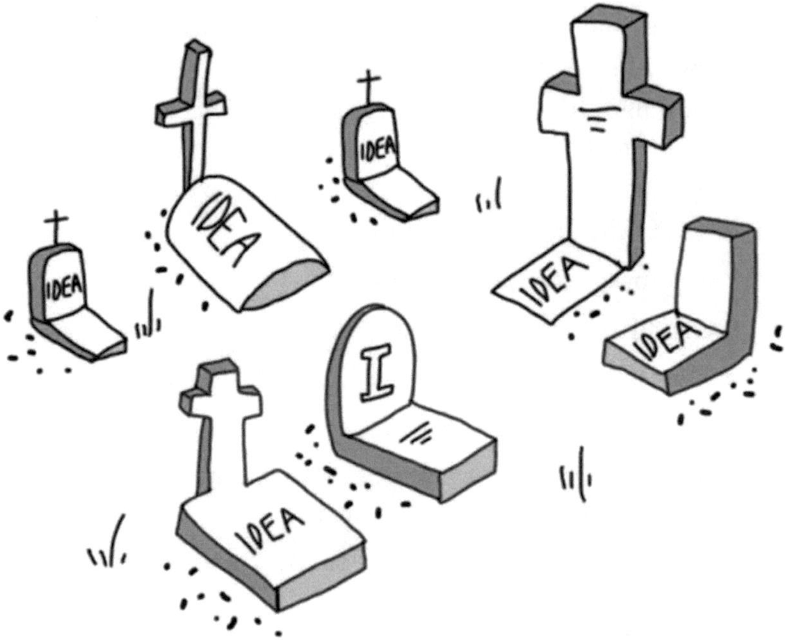
IDEA
IDEA
IDEA
IDEA
IDEA
I
IDEA

IDEAS

*The person who makes something today
isn't the same person who returns
to the work tomorrow.*
—Rick Rubin, The Creative Act

One day, a friend came over to visit and walked into my home office for the first time.

"What are those?" he asked, pointing to a bookshelf filled with dozens of black, purple, and red notebooks.

"That's my idea cemetery."

He looked at me, puzzled.

"All the ideas that didn't make it," I ruefully replied.

It is healthy to have an idea cemetery.

It can be a special place to visit once in a while, to bring proverbial flowers to, and to reflect on what originally inspired those ideas.

Ideas come at various times for different reasons.

It helps to examine them through the present lens and understand that not all ideas are meant to live.

Most should rest in peace.

However, sometimes, when you visit the idea cemetery, something *does* come back to life.

Like this book.

DREAMS (A POEM)

Silence, bones dry
the desert, heart cold
the valley, waiting
brazen, burdensome circle
endings, beginnings,
endings

to be sure, there will be darkness
roads chiseled with safety (regret)
woods gnarled, poisoned (k)nots
the whispers of a hundred hells

this hero's journey
call to wild, waning wonder,
wandering uncertain steps marked out
for timing and taking

it's not the coming true that fills
the unrealism of pursuit
but the hours of days stacked upon years,
built on raw mortar of intention
ethereal, unrealistic, audacious
deep seeds of dreaming
hard harvest, rains of vanity or vision
fortitude for the flickering finite and for
something that was not there (before)

take the chance, O dreamer
the sun of life orbits but once and
the moon of faith shines full

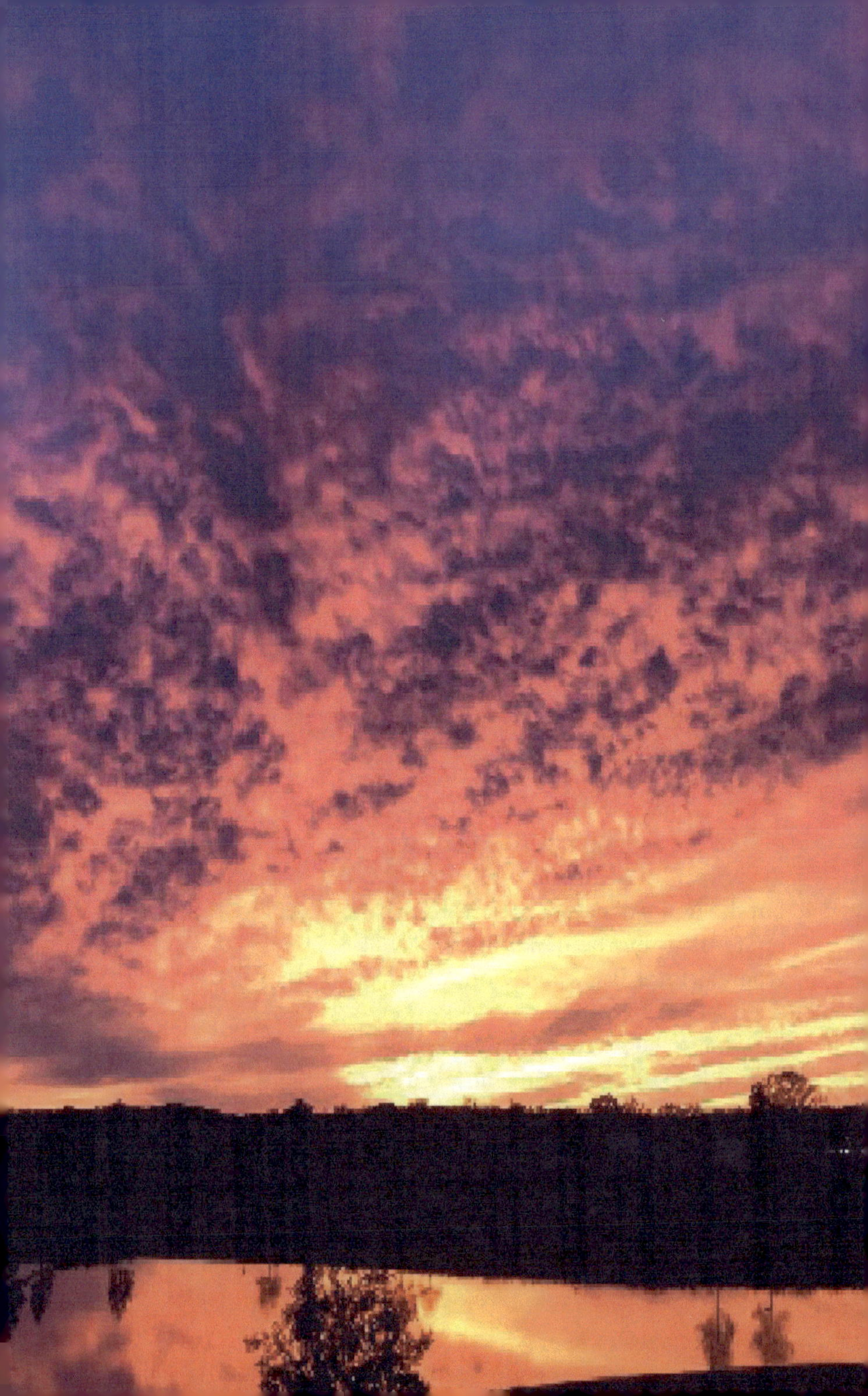

MOMENTARY ART

The sunsets in Georgia rival anything I've been fortunate enough to see from California to New Zealand.

We find stunning landscapes outside our house, a canvas in the sky painted with oranges, purples, pinks, and yellows dappled against large, dramatic clouds. I was so taken with these sunsets (and sunrises that I created a coffee table book filled with photographs, capturing a year's worth of these one-of-a-kind paintings).

If you look away momentarily, the painting changes, morphs, and darkens.

A few minutes later, that singular art in the sky vanishes.

Recently, my family was on St. Simons, an island off the coast of Georgia where my mother grew up. Walking along the beach, we saw an impressive sandcastle. The next day, on the same walk, the sandcastle was gone, washed away by high tide.

I was struck by the pleasure the creators must have had constructing something of beauty meant to vanish within hours.

Yesterday, our curious ten-year-old daughter, Georgia, asked how I make coffee (she is a budding coffee lover).

I was ready for my afternoon cappuccino, so the inquiry was perfectly timed. Besides, anything related to coffee gets me as energized as the caffeine itself.

I showed Georgia how we grind beans, tamp grounds, and froth milk. I also explained the subtle nuances between a latte, cortado, and cappuccino.

Before enjoying the cappuccino, I tried to make a "G" in the coffee, my daughter's initial, my meager attempt at coffee art.

Then it was gone.

Sunsets, sandcastles, and coffee designs are all temporary art whose beauty is found only in the present, in a few magical moments.

Some things in life do not require an outcome or result.

They require our attention.

We honor timeless masterpieces that are forever displayed in museums and galleries worldwide. Still, we often miss the present moments of a tree in full bloom before its leaves drop, an incredible meal prepared by a passionate chef, or live music in your favorite venue.

A conversation between friends or partners can be artful. Two humans creating meaningful dialogue for a moment can have an impact forever.

There is beauty in the temporary.

We must learn not to consume beauty but to consummate it, perfecting the experience until it is gone.

There will never be one like it again. I challenge us to go through a day discovering the momentary art in our lives.

The art is there.
We need to take a **moment** and look for it.

Joe Castillo has built his career around momentary art.

Using light and sand, he creates amazing masterpieces that are here for a moment, then wiped away. For over thirty years, Joe has performed around the world creating momentary art.

To learn more about Joe and his SandStory art, please visit:
joecastillo.com

REALITY

Reality is the debt I pay for the dreams I chase.

INSPIRATION

I only write when I am inspired.
Fortunately, I am inspired every morning at 9:00 a.m.
—William Faulkner

(could be ascribed to W. Somerset Maugham)

What inspires you?

How do you inspire others?

What are you willing to **show up for, regardless of whether** you feel inspired or not?

PERSEVERANCE

It's not that I'm so smart.
It's just that I stay with problems longer.
—Albert Einstein

I cannot tell you how many times I have wanted to give up.

There have been many seasons of wandering bare, arid land without inspiration, encouragement, or creative fulfillment.

The bright daybreak bursts of inspiration and encouragement have followed dark nights of the soul.

Looking back, I am grateful for those seasons, hard as they were (and as hard as they will continue to be).

Our path to Ithaka is never a straight line.

The winds of life blow us off course.

We shipwreck.

Pirates invade.

There are powerful squalls.

Sometimes we capsize.

And occasionally, we sink.

How we survive and when we arrive cannot happen without the art of perseverance.

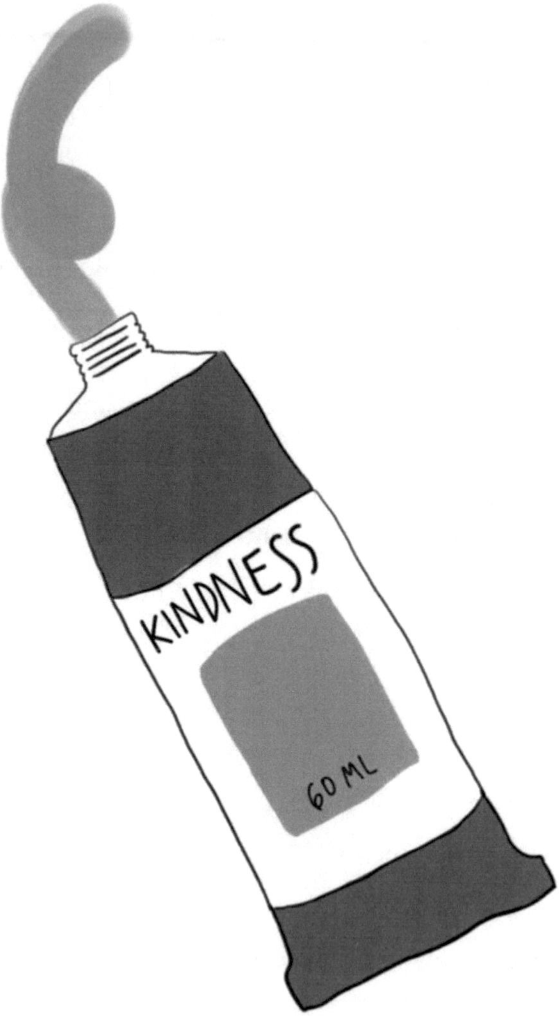
KINDNESS
60 ML

KINDNESS

Now, the million-dollar question:
Why aren't we kinder? – George Saunders

Saunders is a best-selling author. In his book *Congratulations, by the Way*, which is based on a convocation speech he delivered to Syracuse University, this self-proclaimed "old fart" has gathered thoughts about kindness into one book.

"What I regret most in my life are failures of kindness," Saunders says. *"I can look back and see that I have spent much of my life in a cloud of things that have tended to push "being kind" to the periphery. Things like anxiety. Fear. Insecurity. Ambition. The mistaken belief that if I can only accrue enough—enough accomplishment, money, fame—my neuroses will disappear.*

Over the years, I've felt kindness, sure—but let me finish this semester, this degree, this book; let me succeed at this job, afford the house, and raise the kids, and then, finally, when all is accomplished, I'll get started on the kindness."

Where have I failed to be kind? Where have I traded kindness for ambition, neuroses, and accomplishment?

We tell our daughters that no matter how messy the day ends, each morning brings new mercy in the form of a blank canvas with fresh paint.

We get to begin again, painting a new day, using one of the most vibrant paint colors we have available—**kindness.**

100

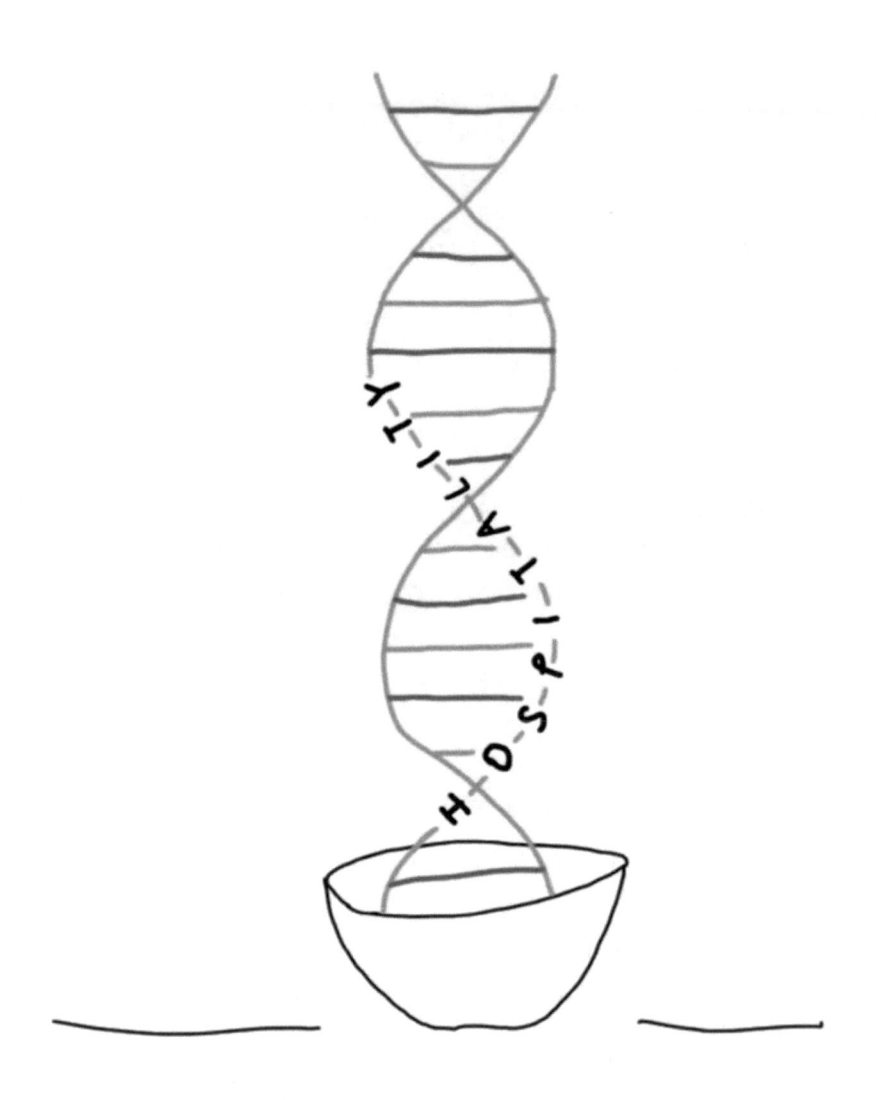

PHO

When Jack Louneoubonh serves you a bowl of his delicious pho: he is not just serving you a meal; he is telling you a story. This story began in a refugee camp in Thailand during the Vietnam War.

At three years old, Jack's journey was anything but clear when his Laotian father and Thai mother fled the war with him and his brother, coming to the United States in the early 1980s. They landed in San Diego, where an American family gracefully sponsored them through their church.

Jack's family lived in California for five years before moving to Washington. There, amongst other Asian refugees, his parents labored in a meat processing plant. The work was hard and inconsistent, and did not pay well. Although they suffered financially, they could still provide for their family as best as they could. When the factory closed, the family sought work wherever it could be found. They moved from Florida to Georgia to Nebraska and finally back to Georgia, where they eventually settled.

Jack was a curious child with an uncanny knack for learning quickly. He learned to speak English by watching American television shows like *Bugs Bunny*, *GI Joe*, and *Transformers*. He eventually excelled in school and sports.

Naturally gregarious, Jack had a penchant for building relationships and engaged with anyone he met. Even today, he says he has met some wonderful people and that God continues introducing him to more amazing people daily.

Jack's humble beginnings, nomadic childhood, and impeccable family work ethic placed him on a lifepath filled with faith, friendship, and hospitality.

"Hospitality was in our DNA," he says. "The love and unity my parents had with our community while cooking will always stick with me."

Although the family didn't have much, they were able to host and cook for a big crowd. This was incredibly special to them and became a defining trait that followed Jack throughout his life.

Jack has been married to Theary, a talented wedding photographer, for seventeen years. He has worked many jobs to help provide for their three children. Although he knew he was where he was supposed to be with any given job, the work never fully expressed his creativity.

Jack's purpose and passion began to align when he was compelled to leave his job as a car dealership manager. His inherited love for cooking pushed him to take a substantial entrepreneurial risk and start a pop-up business—Jack's Poppin' Pho.

Working over large cauldrons of savory broth, Jack prepares food representing his culture and heart.

"The intimacy of building relationships with strangers through my food is beautiful," Jack declares. "The money may come, or it may not, but the significance of taking this step has been well worth the risk."

Jack never questioned his purpose or place despite a rough and uncertain life. His road to Ithaka has led him to where he can finally share a side of himself that he has desired to express for so long.

"I don't regret how my journey has played out. I take it as a gift from God," Jack says. "My faith has allowed me to reflect on everything and realize it was all for a purpose."

If you are ever in Atlanta, seek a hearty, fragrant bowl.

You won't be disappointed with the food or regret meeting Jack in Jack's Poppin' Pho.

instagram.com/jackspoppinpho

ARRIVING THERE

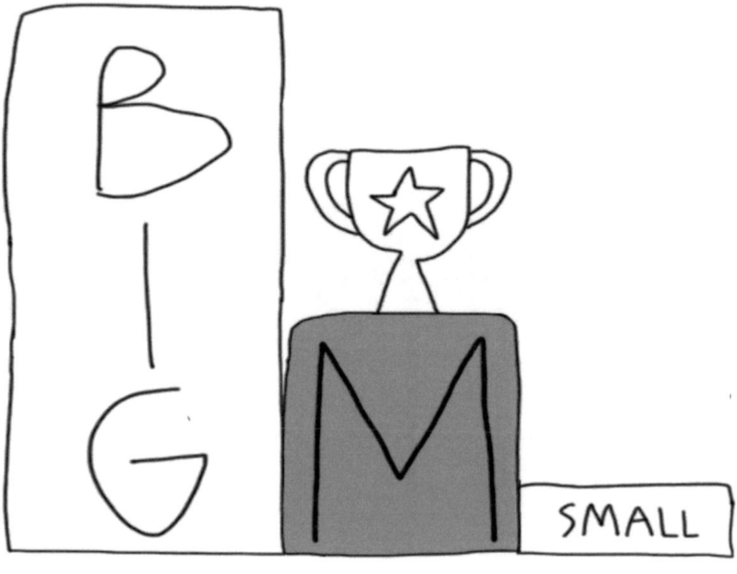
BIG
M
SMALL

MAKE IT MEDIUM

You're not going to make it big.
You're going to make it medium.
—Uncle Bruce

My uncle, Dr. Bruce J. Walz, is a renowned radiologist in St. Louis. Years ago, when my wife and I were first married, Uncle Bruce visited New York City for a medical conference and offered to take us to dinner.

Both struggling artists, we were thrilled to accept the invitation to dinner and spend time with one of the smartest and kindest men on the planet.

At dinner, I blabbered on and on about all the great things I planned on doing in life.

Uncle Bruce listened intently over a delicious meal at a restaurant in SoHo.

Eventually, when I shut my mouth, Uncle Bruce looked me squarely in the eyes and calmly proclaimed:

> ***"Michael, you're not going to make it big.***
> ***You're going to make it medium."***

I shifted uncomfortably in my seat. *Wait, what?*

The restaurant endured the tragic sound of my ego being crushed. Thoughts swirled through my head.

How could he say something like this?

We spent the rest of dinner in awkward conversation. On the subway ride home, my wife knew my spirit was bruised and gently encouraged me.

I am the biggest dreamer in the world, as anyone close to me knows.

Dreaming *big* is an imperative ingredient to success. It is a critical part of the human experience.

I replayed those words for many years, especially when formidable opponents (rejection, doubt, and insecurity reared their ugly heads. Sometimes, I wrestled with resentment in dark, lonely moments when success and achievement seemed most unattainable.

Many years later, we moved to Los Angeles for a season of starting. My wife started her acting career. We started a family. I started a business.

In that business, I had the privilege of taking care of some of the wealthiest people in the world—ultra-high-net-worth individuals and families who had *really* made it big. I navigated the psychology of success as I peeked through a unique portal into serious ambition and accomplishment.

It looked great on paper. But it wasn't always pretty.

Through our creative communities and the clients I serve, I continue to learn that "making it big" often has a dark side. It frequently involves trading something of intrinsic value for something else of extrinsic value.

This often tragic trade-off occurs when we least perceive it. At some point, we choose (intentionally or unintentionally) to trade our relationships, health, marriage, integrity, and perhaps soul in exchange for something bigger or better.

This is usually *more* of anything—power and money, influence and status, awards and leverage. Eventually, an even more tragic exchange unfolds. One then tries to use their money, power, and influence to repurchase the very things they traded in the first place. I say "tries" because this is not a fungible process. These values are not mutually interchangeable.

Faustian story after story, well-meaning individuals and companies trade something of priceless value for something else that may or may not be worth the trade. From Robert Johnson, the famed blues musician who allegedly traded his soul for his musical mastery, to any Hollywood marriages that ended in public disaster, somebody traded who or what they had for something bigger, someone better.

Many trials, ups and downs, wins and losses later, my father passed away. This was a primary catalyst for us to move back to Georgia to be closer to family and friends while growing new roots in the southern soil on which we were raised.

And it was here, on a sunny morning in Georgia, that I woke up with a bold revelation:

Maybe Uncle Bruce was right!

Could making it medium mean making it big?

Perhaps dreaming big and making it big are two different things.

And what are we making, after all? A living or a life?

What do we do with the tension between pursuing our dreams and preserving our values?

Can we dream big and realize those dreams without trading what matters most? Do they have to be mutually independent?

What if we could achieve our dreams while keeping our relationships, marriage, friendships, health, and integrity (soul) in place?

What is the difference between a trade-off and a sacrifice?

How do we create margin to get the most from our work?

What if we could recalibrate success by redefining our own definition?

Uncle Bruce had a noble idea: **make it medium.**

MAPS AND COMPASSES

Years ago, I wrote a screenplay with a line that over time has proven not to be that original, but still true in my experience:

Some people are born with a map.
Others are born with a compass.

I am 100% a compass person. I subscribe to the J.R.R. Tolkien philosophy of, "Not all who wander are lost."

I have always preferred an adventure.

With my compass in hand, I would wander until the needle pointed in a direction that made sense—okay, I guess this is where I am going now and what I am doing next.

The truth is, my life sometimes would have been much easier at times if I just used the map.

I know and love many map people.

And I bet some of them wished they had used a compass once in a while instead.

Either way, both are used for the same purpose:

Navigation

We all have a unique way to get to where we are going.

Let's not judge others based on their navigational tools.

We are all doing our best to get there.

We all lose our way every once in a while. We all get lost.

But sometimes—when we are lost—that is when we find what we need most.

*I don't know where I am going,
but I know how to get there.*

—Boyd Varty, lion tracker

SLOWLY IS THE FASTEST WAY

Andre De Shields has been working in theater for over 50 years. In 2019, at seventy-three years old, he won a Tony-Award for Best Performance in a "Featured Role in a Musical" in *Hadestown*.

In his acceptance speech, Andre shared his secrets to longevity in the arts:

1. Surround yourself with people whose eyes light up when they see you coming.
2. Slowly is the fastest way to get to where you want to be.
3. The top of one mountain is the bottom of the next, so keep climbing.

I think about all the activities in my life that I rushed through for expediency and efficiency, activities and engagements that were never meant to be rushed but to be savored and enjoyed.

Slowly. Deliberately. Intentionally.

A meal my wife takes an hour to prepare is devoured in ten minutes.

A leisurely morning walk becomes a jog so I can return home to work on things that make me need *another* walk.

A prayer evolves into a checklist I rapidly move through to return to "more important things."

We scroll through life like an Instagram feed, mindlessly searching for something that will interest us just enough to pause for that momentary dopamine-filled jolt.

And then we keep scrolling.

We spend more time getting lost in the rabbit holes of life, engaging with one-dimensional, ideological human beings on a screen, than we do connecting and conversing with real humans at a dinner table.

It's a trap.

We need to slow down.

As Simon and Garfunkel said in the *59th Street Bridge Song*, we have to make our mornings last.

Take the slow route.

It's the fastest way to Ithaka.

Bad things can happen fast,
but almost all good things happen *slowly*.
—Kevin Kelly

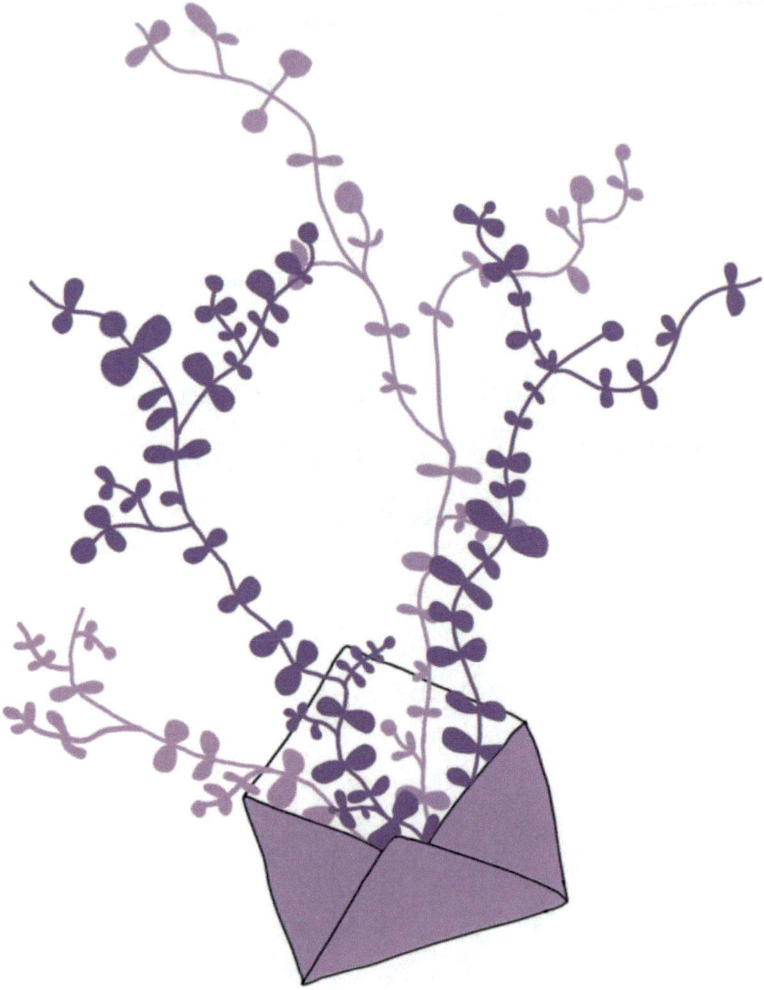

THE ENVELOPE

One Saturday evening years ago, I received a call from one of my favorite clients.

As usual, he had a special assignment for me.

He and his wife had gone to the movies in suburban Las Vegas earlier that evening, and he explained that a young man was working at the theater who was disabled. He asked me to find out what I could about the young man and, when I had that information, to fly out to Las Vegas to meet with him.

I did my reconnaissance and discovered that the young man's name was Daniel and that he only worked on Saturday nights. So, the following Saturday, I flew from Los Angeles to Las Vegas, rented a car, and drove to my client's home. As I waited in the foyer of his home, he came down the stairs with an envelope in his hand.

"This is ten thousand dollars cash," he said as he handed me the envelope. "I want you to go to the movie theater, find Daniel, and tell him that you represent somebody who thinks he does a great job. Then hand him the envelope."

My instructions were clear.

So, I drove to the movie theater to fulfill the mission. Of course, it was Las Vegas, and the lobby was a labyrinth of slot machines I had to navigate through to get to the entrance.

And once I did, there was Daniel, working diligently, tearing tickets as customers entered.

I will be honest. I was really emotional at this point.

I was also nervous with that much cash in my pocket. I ducked into the bathroom to take a few deep breaths. When I exited, I walked right up to Daniel.

"Daniel," I said, "I represent somebody who thinks you do a great job. And he wants to gift you." I handed him the envelope, quickly turned around, left the theater, drove back to the airport, and flew home to Los Angeles.

My client never saw Daniel's reaction when he opened the envelope, so he never experienced how this gift transformed his life.

But that was *never* the point. He wanted to give a gift, express appreciation, and show respect.

Daniel was the unsuspecting recipient, and I, the conduit of generosity.

Generosity is a powerful force.

It has the energy to change lives and create new stories.

It can be radical and anonymous.

It also can be so very simple.

If we cultivate a culture of generosity in our lives, sometimes we will be the giver, sometimes the receiver, and every once in a while . . .

. . . we get to deliver the envelope.

I STILL HAVEN'T FOUND WHAT I'M LOOKING FOR

My childhood friend Nick, a lifelong U2 aficionado, boldly committed these letters to tattoos on each of his fingers.

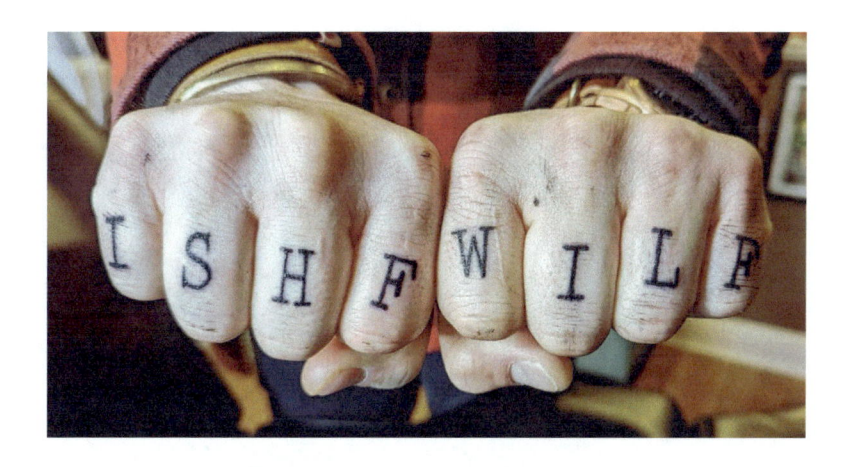

Many are looking for something.

Few have found it.

What are *you* looking for?

If you found it, would it fulfill?

Would it be everything you thought it would be?

What are you so committed to finding that you would tattoo it on your body?

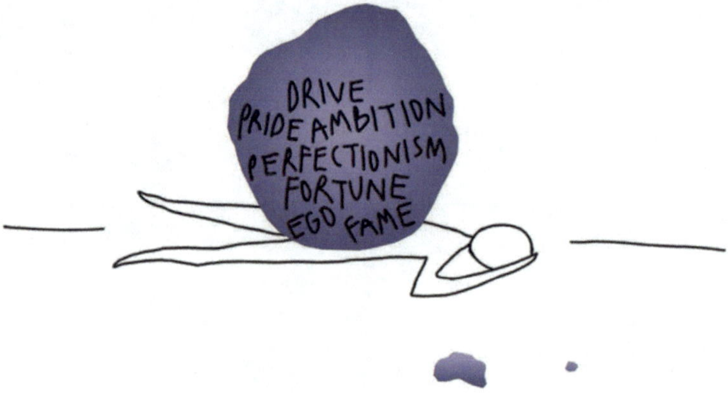
DRIVE
PRIDE AMBITION
PERFECTIONISM
FORTUNE
EGO FAME

ARRIVING

Arriving to Ithaka is our destiny/destination.

It's where we are heading.

However, many arrived there too early and tragically didn't stay long. These are a few of the well-known souls that arrived before their time.

River Phoenix (died at 23)

James Dean (died at 24)

Kurt Cobain (died at 27)

Amy Winehouse (died at 27)

Jimi Hendrix (died at 27)

Heath Ledger (died at 28)

Jeff Buckley (died at 30)

Bob Marley (died at 36)

Elvis Presley (died at 42)

Whitney Houston (died at 48)

Michael Jackson (died at 50)

Many others hurried the journey and arrived too soon only to learn that their drive, pride, ambition, ego, perfectionism, fortune, and fame were crushing weights they were not meant to carry.

Here is where you are meant to be.
There is where you are headed.
But don't hurry the journey at all.

At the right time, your ... *there* ... will be here.

All that glitters is not gold.
—Shakespeare, The Merchant of Venice

ENDURING

***Better if it lasts for years, so you're old
by the time you reach the island . . .***

Willie Nelson will be ninety-one years old in 2024.

Robert Duvall is ninety-three.

Clint Eastwood is ninety-four (this stud is still creating).

So is Gene Hackman.

Mel Brooks is ninety-eight.

Dick Van Dyke will be ninety-nine in December 2024.

We recently lost Angela Lansbury, Sidney Poitier, Bob Barker, Barbara Walters, Estelle Harris, Tony Bennet, Loretta Lynn, Gena Rowlands (just in August 2024), James Earl Jones (RIP, he just passed in September 2024), and Norman Lear. They were all in their 90s except Lear. He was 101.

Just yesterday, a relative of William Kennedy told me that the Pulitzer Prize-winning author of Ironweed is ninety-six years old and writes in his home office every day, without fail (Christmas included).

Many other artists whose names are less well-known continue to create and produce art well into their 90s and even into their 100s.

Carmen de Lavallade—an American choreographer and who continued to perform and create new works into her 90s.

Lenore Tawney—an American fiber artist who continued to create and exhibit her textile works into her 90s. She died at 100.

Ruth Asawa—an American sculptor who continued to create wire sculptures into her 80s and was recognized for her contributions to American art.

Louise Bourgeois was a French-American sculptor who continued to create and exhibit her work into her 90s. She was known for her large-scale installations and sculptures. She passed away at ninety-eight.

Proof positive from these artists: creativity, passion, and artistic talent can continue to flourish well into life's journey.

Their works are a testament to the enduring power of the human spirit and the mysterious nature of creating art and life.

Sometimes, age is just a number that attempts to define our limitations.

Francis Ford Coppola, at eighty-five years old, recently finished production of his latest film, *Megalopolis*.

Shot mostly in our neighborhood, it is a story Coppola has been dreaming of telling for over four decades. A film some, including himself, consider his magnum opus.

My family had the opportunity to visit the wildly futuristic film set. It was so inspiring to get a short glimpse of this seasoned master at work.

It reminded me that no matter how old we are, we should:

Keep working.
Keep dreaming.
Keep serving.
Keep **enduring**.

Our greatest work could be right ahead.

STAMINA

ENTHUSIASM +
PATIENCE −
EXPECTATIONS =
STAMINA

$$E + P - X = S$$

HALF

Hope your road is a long one.
May there be many summer mornings when,
with what pleasure, what joy,
you enter harbors you're seeing for the first time.

If what they say about coffee and its antioxidant benefits are true, I should live past 100 years old.

But, of course, I cannot control this.

My days are numbered. So are yours.

Assuming I am fortunate to live to a ripe old age, my life is half over.

It is difficult for me to admit. Thinking of your life as half over is both sobering *and* inspiring.

My friend Daniel is an artist, a beautiful, soulful singer and songwriter. A few years ago, he turned me on to Richard Rohr's *Falling Upward: A Spirituality for the Two Halves of Life.*

Where I challenge some of Rohr's theological principles, the book explores the two distinct yet interconnected halves of life.

We invest in pursuing ambition, security, and success in the first half.

The second half is where we embark on a spiritual transformation and growth journey, releasing our ego and letting go of our illusions and attachments.

Ideally, we redirect our self-focus toward others through acts of service and love.

Who we were when we began our journey will not be who we are when we arrive.

There will be different versions of ourselves along the way.

Different relationships.

Different seasons.

Different dreams.

Circumstances.

Challenges.

Perspectives.

> We were meant to thrive and not just survive.
> We are glad when someone survives,
> and that surely takes some courage and effort.
> But what are you going to do with your now resurrected life?
> That is the heroic question.
>
> —Richard Rhor, *Falling Upward*

Here is an interesting study on the health benefits of coffee:

Wang Y, Li H, Wang W, et al. Coffee Drinking and Mortality in 10 European Countries: A Multinational Cohort Study. Annals of Internal Medicine. 2021;174(4):505-514. doi:10.7326/M20-5143

The journey always changes.
The journey always changes us.

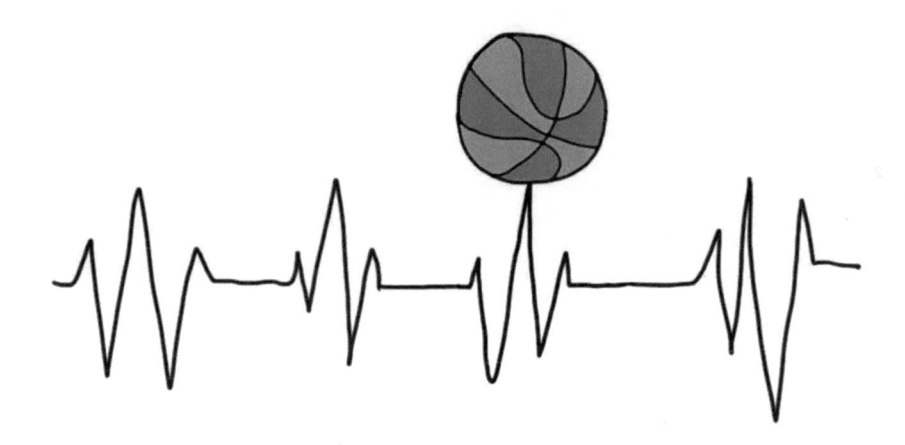

THEY'RE AGGRESSIVE

The process of learning basketball is never complete. There is always something new to learn, something to improve upon.

—Jerry West, fourteen-time NBA All-Star (and the iconic figure on the NBA's logo)

In the summer of 2020, when the world was shut down due to Covid, I was walking in my burgeoning neighborhood in South Atlanta. I walked past a newly built community basketball court.

I stopped for a moment, thinking to myself that I had never seen anyone use the court.

I went home and, like with everything else we needed during shelter-in-place, purchased a basketball on Amazon.

When the basketball arrived, I went to the court and thought to myself:

*Okay, **this** ball goes into **that** orange rim with a net.*

I attempted a few shots and went home.

I went back the next day and took a few more shots than the day before.

This practice continued until I started to enjoy the meditative repetition. I had no form, function, experience, or intellectual understanding of how the game was even played.

But I showed up to the court almost every day.

One Saturday morning, I went down to shoot some baskets, and ten guys were running full-court games. One of them was my neighbor, Rashad Hodge.

Rashad is a former Army member who played football at West Point (and, as I would later learn the hard way, played basketball like he played football).

He is a big, strong, disciplined teddy bear of a man. And he is a world-class, I mean **world-class** trash talker. The things he has said to me on the court have made me cry for my mother.

I watched these guys run up and down the court.

It looked fun. And exhausting.

A week later, I ran into Rashad and used the opportunity to step out of my comfort zone. I asked him if I could play basketball with him and his friends. He was cordial and enthusiastic. On the other hand, his lovely wife lowered her sunglasses and plainly stated, "They're aggressive."

"That's okay," I replied. "I'd still love to play."

Rashad invited me to join him that following Saturday at 7:00 a.m. Friday night, I tossed and turned in bed, riddled with anxiety.

What was I thinking?! Why did I commit to this!?
I am a writer, not an athlete!

But I am also a man of my word.

I got up early, drank coffee, prayed, and was on the court at 6:45 a.m.

Rashad showed up a few minutes later. We shot around and made small talk before the rest of the players arrived.

We picked teams and started to play.

It was not pretty (I played last night, and it wasn't pretty either).

They ran circles around me. I had no idea what a pick-and-roll was, any more than I did a travel or double dribble (both of which I did, apparently).

I was a lost, confused heap of sweat. And then:

Rashad broke one of my ribs.

I was guarding him, and on a drive toward the basket, he lowered his shoulder, charged through the paint, and went straight into my ribcage. I can't even remember if he made the basket, but I remember the pain. It was brutal. As I gasped for air, the prophetic words of Rashad's wife rattled throughout my head.

They're aggressive.

It took many weeks of healing and many sleepless nights before I would show back to the court.

Broken ribs, severely rolled ankles, a bloodied nose, poked eyes, torn and bruised muscles, a ruptured ear drum, a loose tooth, and jammed fingers resulted in me falling so in love with the game of basketball that my family and friends could hardly believe it.

I play as often as I can and practice even more. I have to work ten times harder than the guys I play with, most of whom are half my age and twice my size. And **so** much better than me.

I share this story because this is one of the rare areas of my life where I am 100% committed to the *journey*, not the destination.

Because there is **no** destination for me with basketball. There is only **journey**.

Ithaka mentions the riches we collect along the way.

For me, these riches are found on the basketball court. The wealth I gain with every practice shot, every game I play, and all the generous coaching my friends, teammates, and opponents offer are far more excellent than a destination I will never reach.

They are found on the road to learning, where I deeply enjoy community, competition, and camaraderie.

I gain this when I play with friends and strangers from diverse backgrounds, ethnicities, and faiths, all bound by the shared passion for a beautiful game.

We speak the love language of basketball.

You won't win every game.

But you will lose every game you don't show up to.

You won't make every shot.

But you will miss every shot you don't take.

The journey to Ithaka will be *aggressive*.

Life will be aggressive. But we still have to show up.

And we have to take our shots.

Then, we do it repeatedly, developing the form and muscle memory required to make the shots count.

We will miss many of them.

But we will miss **all** the shots we don't take.

A special thanks to a few guys in the beginning who patiently coached and encouraged me when I had no idea what I was doing: Adam Glendye, Dom Kegel, Hayden Long, Micheal Thompson, Jamie Waltermire, Jason Jackson, Gabriel Martin, Jesse Lindsley, Jamal Cook, and, of course, Rashad Hodge. Each of you helped me discover the riches in basketball.

NOTHING LEFT TO GIVE

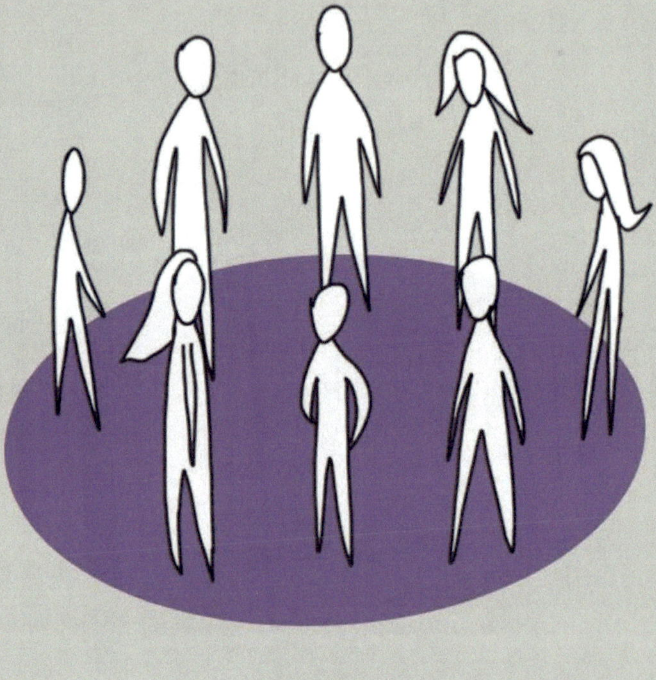

BELONGING

Everybody comes into the world looking for somebody who is looking for them.

—Dr. Curt Thompson, neurologist

It was "picture day" at my high school (shout out to MHS!).

All of the club and organization members gathered in the school courtyard to take photos for the yearbook. The week before, I brought my checkbook (the original **Venmo**) to school and wrote club dues for every possible club I could join.

Debate Club. Chess Club. Key Club. Spanish Club. FCA.

If they had a Knitting Club, I would have paid dues for that club, too.

At the end of the year, I was featured on many pages of the yearbook as a proud member of clubs to which I did not belong. My friends and I got a kick out of it. But something deeper was happening. It was an active search for belonging. I wasted a lot of money on those club dues because I never found what I was looking for.

Until one afternoon, my loyal friend, Jeff Dark, offered to drive me home after school.

You see, I had my car taken away by my father for a month for doing something stupid. Jeff was kind enough to give me a ride so I did not have to make the treacherous one-mile journey on foot. It was not treacherous. I am being dramatic.

Side note: Jeff happened to be the yearbook editor and had to see my face suspiciously show up in all of those club photos I was a "member" of that year.

On the way to my house, Jeff stopped at the high school auditorium to sign up for the fall drama production.

I followed him inside.

On a curious whim, I also signed up for the production.

I had no idea what I was doing. I had never acted before (except for my brief stint as a Secret Serviceman—see "Impostor Syndrome").

I auditioned, landed a part, and won a "Best Actor" award.

When I stepped into the theater for the first rehearsal, I was surrounded by others searching for a place to belong.

I walked in looking for people who were looking for me.

I found them—my tribe—these misfits, storytellers, and theatrical artists. Around them and in that space, I felt I could thrive for the first time in my young adult life.

The alchemy and sense of belonging are profound when we find the people trying to find us. However, the consequences of not belonging are profoundly devastating.

- As recently as June 2023, one study published in the journal PLOS Medicine cited that loneliness has far-reaching consequences and the health impact is comparable to smoking up to fifteen cigarettes a day!
- Social isolation and loneliness have been linked to a 29% increase in heart disease and a 32% risk of stroke.
- People who are socially isolated are more likely to have weakened immune systems and can increase the risk of illness and infection.
- A study in 2020 found that social isolation and loneliness were associated with a 50% increased risk of developing dementia.

- A study in 2021 found that social isolation was associated with an increased risk of suicidal ideation and attempts among college students during the Covid-19 pandemic.
- A 2018 study found that approximately one in five adults in the United States reported feeling lonely and socially isolated. That's 20% of our population do not feel they belong.

The studies and risks go on and on.

Belonging is not a modern buzzword. It is ancient and anthropological. If you were kicked out of your tribe, it meant isolation and death. If you don't find your tribe today, it could also mean isolation and death.

Humanity depends on belonging. In today's post-Covid, disconnected world, we seek belonging in all the wrong places.

The journey to Ithaka can often be lonely.

But it doesn't have to be.

Make sure you find a safe place where you belong.

Your survival and mental health depend on your tribe; others will depend on you to be a part of theirs.

And as we change, sometimes so do our tribes.

People will come into your life for a reason, a season, or forever.

Everything can change in a moment.

Even our tribes.

But what never changes is our *need* for **belonging**.

Where and with whom do you feel you most belong?

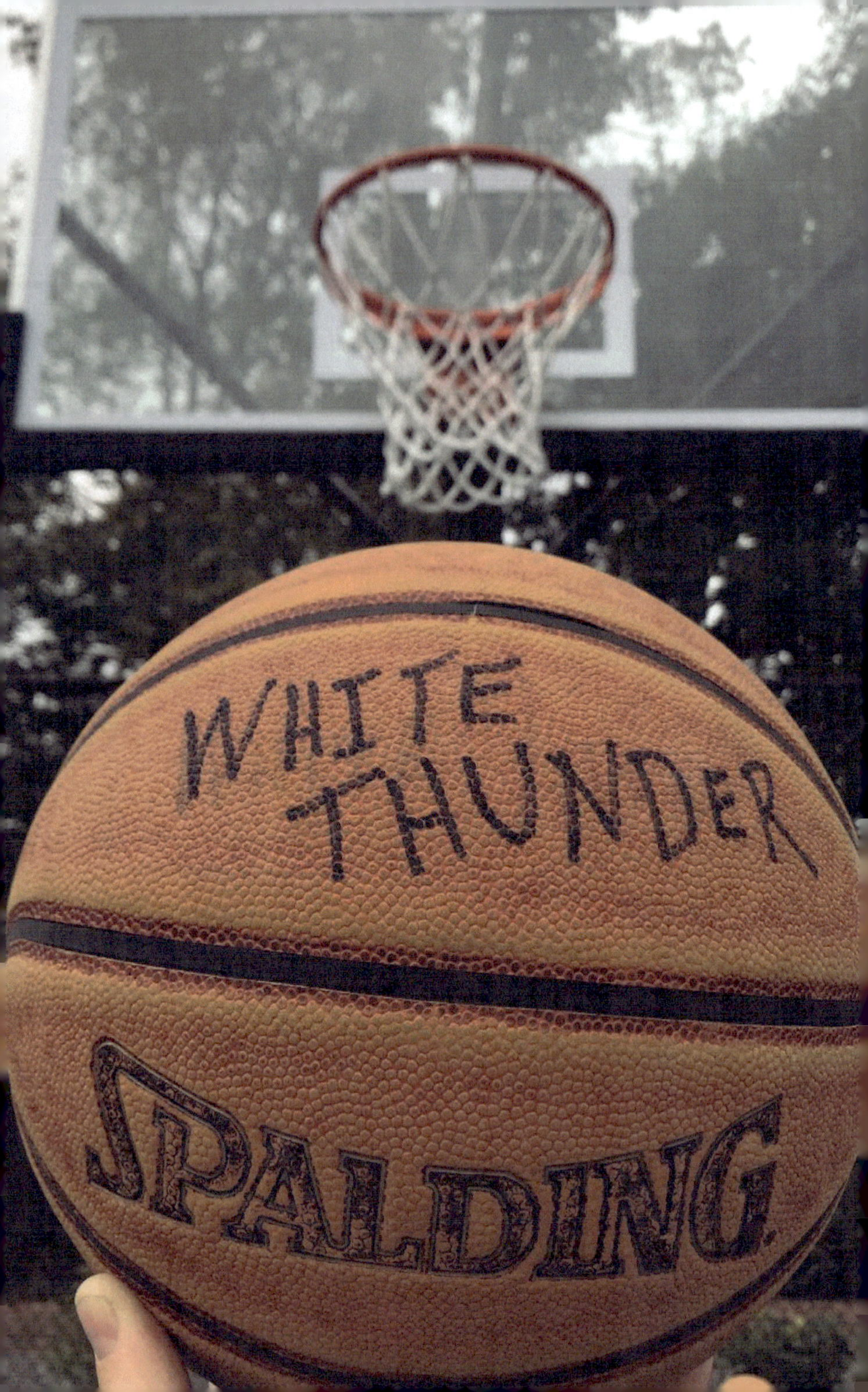
WHITE
THUNDER
SPALDING

FOULS TO GIVE

In basketball, as in the game of life, we must show up every day prepared to play both offense and defense.

We must bring everything we have learned in practice to the game, including:

- Sportsmanship
- Awareness
- Conditioning
- Selflessness
- Honesty
- Respect
- Teamwork
- Ability
- Communication
- Confidence
- IQ
- Consistency
- Mental toughness
- Hustle
- Coachability
- Integrity
- Strategy
- Adaptability
- Agility
- Responsibility
- Versatility
- Flexibility
- And maybe ... a little trash-talking

And every day, we get to practice the game of life.

Each game, the team is limited in the number of fouls they can commit before reaching the penalty.

When we reach the penalty and commit too many fouls, our opponent is awarded free, open shots.

Life will always take those free shots.

It's going to play dirty.

It will talk trash.

It has unlimited fouls to give.

Life will rough you up in the paint, and you might get an elbow to the ribs.

You will bend over, hands on your knees, out of breath, praying for a time out.

And then you will be back on the court.

But remember, *you* also have fouls to give in any given game. Don't be afraid to use them. You always take the high road and never fight back dirty. But you can use a foul to disrupt your opponent's momentum or rhythm to stop them from scoring.

Draw up your plan for each game, each day.

Because life is drawing up plans of its own.

It is carefully and methodically watching your tape.

It knows how you move, think, and act.

It knows how you have played in the past and counts on you making the same plays.

Or mistakes.

You have fouls to give.

Use them.

And use them wisely.

Your shot clock hasn't expired yet.

FOREVER YOUNG

May you build a ladder to the stars and climb on every rung.
—Bob Dylan

Bob Dylan is one of the greatest living poets.

That is my opinion, of course.

His songs (all songs) are poems.

As I thought about this book, I realized that many of Dylan's most popular songs capture the themes I wanted to explore here: dreaming, enduring, working, and changing.

His songs are filled with encouragement. To be strong. To be brave. To follow your heart no matter the obstacles.

"Forever Young" is a catchy and folksy song encouraging us to remain young at heart, be filled with dreams and hope, and never give up, even amid life's challenges.

"Like a Rolling Stone" explores endurance.

"All Along the Watchtower" explores uncertainty.

"Don't Think Twice, It's All Right" is about letting go, moving on, and embracing change.

"Blowin' in the Wind" provokes us to keep asking questions and never give up on our journey to a better world.

"The Times They Are A-Changin'" is an anthem of protest for political and social change, to stand up for what we believe in so our collective future will be brighter.

These are not just songs.

They are a way of life.

They are poetic paths to purpose and meaning.

There is power in the stories songs tell.

If the world is meant to be left better than we found it, then like Bob Dylan said . . . we need to keep on keepin' on.

Is anyone as excited as I am about *A Complete Unknown*, James Mangold's upcoming film about Bob Dylan?!

TERMS AND CONDITIONS

When we engage in a contract or agreement, we sign off on terms and conditions.

We typically agree to an average of ten to thirty pages of T&Cs for social media platforms. In addition to their terms and conditions, there are a litany of privacy policies, data collection, and community guidelines.

As of the writing of this book, Twitter's (sorry, X's) terms of service are fourteen pages long, Instagram's is seventeen pages long, and Verizon Wireless's customer agreement is twenty-eight pages long.

What about financial institutions? Wells Fargo's consumer account fee and information schedule has forty pages of text covering a wide range of riveting topics, from overdraft protection to electronic funds transfers and account fees.

All are written in legalese, a mindless and boring parlance that *we never read.*

But just because we don't read it does not mean it is unimportant.

We willingly agree. We click boxes and sign dotted lines.

We agree to somebody else's terms and conditions, which are in *their* best interests, not ours.

My friend, Denise Spatafora, who is an entrepreneur, consultant, and inspiring soul said something to me a long time ago that has resonated ever since:

Design your life on your terms.

I thought about this for a long time until it meaningfully sunk in. She allowed me to take agency over my life and design it with specific terms and conditions *I* created.

This was transformative.

I started to look at my life as a blueprint for something that could be built using my unique engineering, architecture, and design elements. I could construct something that agreed to a set of terms and conditions uniquely crafted for *my* life. I started to write out my terms and conditions, a binding agreement with myself.

Will you let somebody else map out your life based on where *they* want you to go? If you agree, your terms and conditions will no longer be yours. You will wander toward a destination never meant to be yours.

Sit down and write out your life's terms and conditions.

Be specific.

Agree *only* to these conditions.

Design your life on these terms.

You do not need permission for this design process.

Make sure this is not somebody else's journey but *yours*.

UNCOMFORTABLE

**The more you seek discomfort,
the more you will become comfortable with discomfort.**
—Conor McGregor

Everyone who knows me knows I don't wear shorts. Even in 100-degree, 100% Georgia humidity.

No shorts.

I have even played basketball in jeans.

And I confess—it's not comfortable.

I thought about why I have this uncomfortable idiosyncrasy. Besides having blindingly white legs and maybe me being a little weird, I realized something deeper was going on.

I thrive in certain levels of discomfort.

If I get too comfortable, I get lazy, and feeling lazy makes me *uncomfortable*. Being in a state of discomfort helps keep me from getting complacent. For me, discomfort helps build grit.

Western culture has become incredibly comfortable. Everything is easier, especially in America.

My children do not know a world where you had to sit through commercials during your favorite show and wait a whole week to see the next episode (like I did on Friday nights with *The Incredible Hulk*).

They do not know a world where you cannot press a button on your phone and the next day, a package arrives on your doorstep.

The discomfort of delayed gratification has been eliminated, leaving heightened expectations and impatience in its wake.

Do I enjoy these modern conveniences? Yes, of course.

After all, we are hardwired for comfort and safety. Being comfortable is a natural default and defense mechanism. It's the comfort zone theory at work, rooted in homeostasis, the fear of the unknown, and the drive toward safety.

Cognitive biases and the desire to maintain stability contribute to our need for and seeking of **comfort.**

Stepping outside the comfort zone can often trigger anxiety and stress, but I found in my own life that it is necessary for personal growth and development.

There will be plenty in this world to make our lives more challenging without us actively seeking hardship. This is more about our purposeful intentions and actions to step out of our comfort zone to grow and develop the gift of grit.

I am rehashing what is commonly known, but stepping outside of our comfort zone is highly individualized and can sometimes look like:

Stand-up comedy
Cold water therapy
Running long distances
Lifting heavy things
Constructive criticism
Reading challenging books
Public speaking

Sitting in the silence

Sitting in the mess

Travel

Learning a new language

Learning a new instrument

Take up a new sport (see "They're Aggressive")

Saying no when you want to say yes

Serving others

Doing the hard thing first

Embracing adversity

A mission trip to a developing country

Make hard things make you better (See "Better")

Forgiving

Stepping out in/or into faith

Attending the first AA meeting

Leaning into challenging conversations

What makes you uncomfortable?

Many thought leaders advocate embracing discomfort to grow physically, mentally, creatively, and spiritually.

Because we are inherently selfish and bent toward self-preservation and comfort, one of the most significant ways to seek healthy discomfort is to serve others.

And while some people experience remarkable and horrible discomfort on their journey to Ithaka, I think I am most **comfortable** in my **uncomfortable** jeans.

*Illustration by Asher (twelve), our
daughter, in response to our conversation*

PULL UP THE ANCHOR

> *Getting over a painful experience is much like crossing monkey bars. You have to let go at some point in order to move forward.*
> —**C.S. Lewis**

Recently, our oldest daughter experienced a great deal of anxiety as she moved into a new school. There were big emotions around this change. The memories of her previous school and classmates were quite fond because they were rooted in strong friendships. She was so anchored to those memories and relationships that she was having difficulty letting go so she could create new ones.

Even for adults, emotions can be overwhelming, if not paralyzing, when we face life changes, planned or unplanned. This could be college, a job, a death, a relationship, or a move.

We talked with our daughter about our life as a boat (or lifeboat) and how sometimes there is a season where we cast our anchor and remain safely in the harbor for some time. This season represents safety, stability, and calm.

There are benefits to anchoring when not moving, but there are dangers to moving while dragging our anchor. In boating terms, this could lead to grounding. The boat can drift and potentially run aground, causing extreme damage, especially in shallow and rocky areas.

Many years ago, I had the opportunity to work for a man named Andy King (who later became an Internet meme for his unique participation in the Fyre Festival disaster documentary).

He chartered several boats annually and took his friends and staff to the Caribbean for two weeks. It was my first and only time at sea for such an extended period. And I never slept as deeply and soundly as I did when anchored overnight in island harbors. I slept well because I felt safe, knowing the anchor kept us from drifting or grounding.

But as in life, we can't stay in the bay forever.

We must pull up our anchors and continue on our journey. But why would we want to leave a place of peace and tranquility? Why depart from the calm state of rocking back and forth with gentle lapping waves?

Because most of life is not spent in one place.

Most of life is spent at sea, where it is constantly changing.

When the sea calls us to uncharted waters, this can be frightening as we explore the unknown.

We often attempt to move forward without first pulling up our anchor.

Our emotional anchors rest at the bottom of our past.

They could be traumas, memories, past seasons sweeter than current seasons, opportunities or relationships that have ended, or unrealized dreams.

Anchors weigh the same whether in the water or in the boat.

It is only when the weight is lifted that we then have the freedom to move again fully.

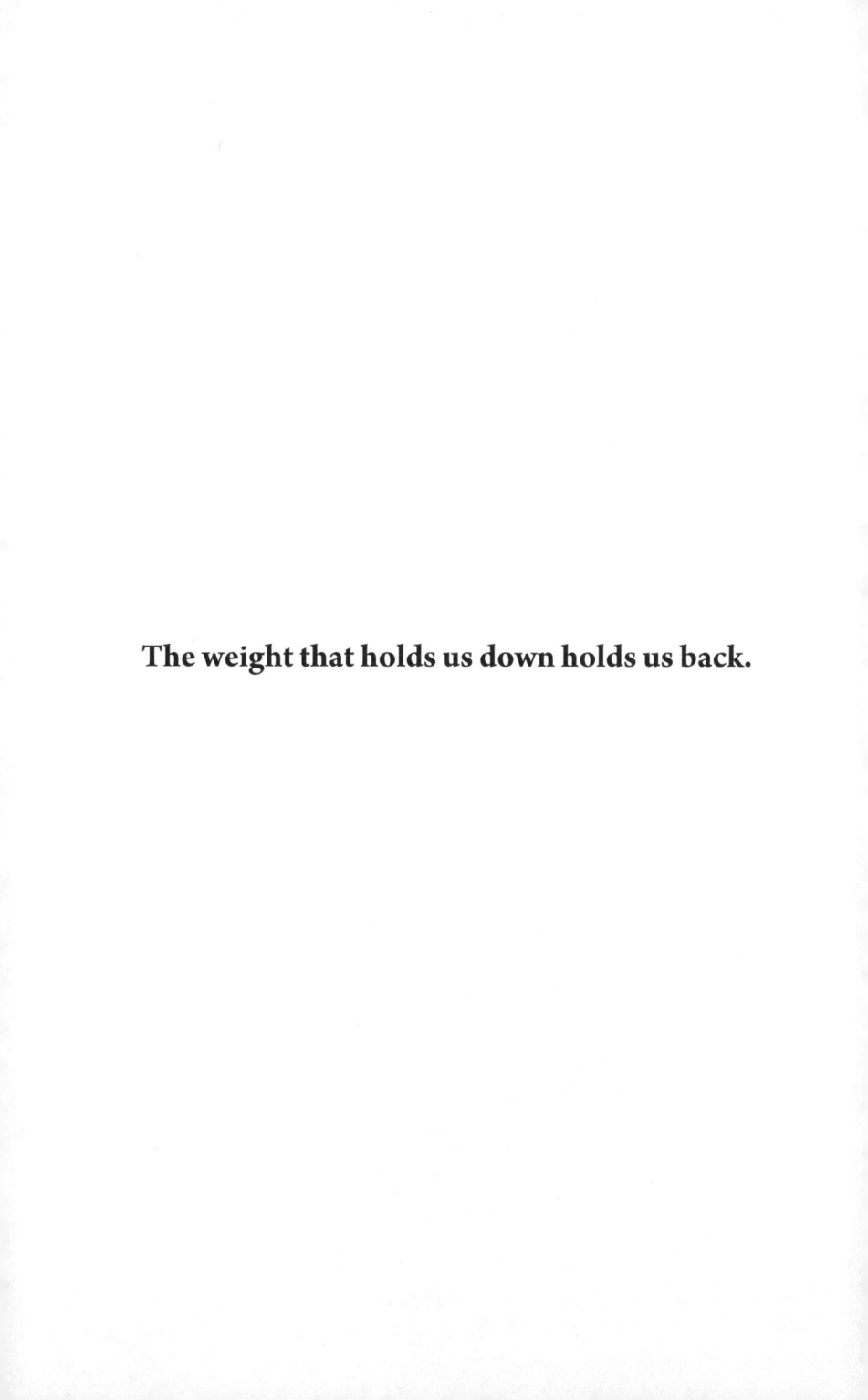

The weight that holds us down holds us back.

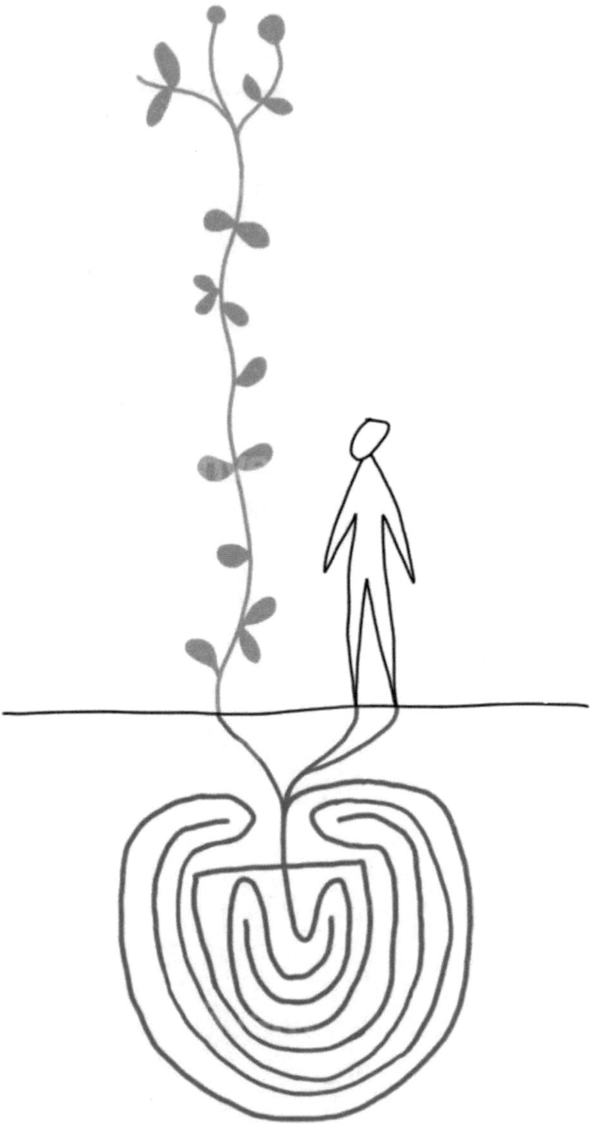

THERE GO I

The Elephant Man is my favorite film.

Directed by David Lynch, this true story is set in 1880's London and chronicles the life and death of Joseph Merrick, a man who suffered extreme deformities of his body and head caused by what doctors believed was neurofibromatosis.

Seedy and greedy showmen paraded Merrick in carnivals throughout England for profit. They would introduced him at sideshows as "one of the most remarkable human beings ever to draw the breath of life."

Indeed, he was.

Over forty years later, this remarkable film profoundly resonates. To this day, when I encounter anybody less fortunate than me, I utter this under my breath:

But for the grace of God, there go I.

I have made this prayerful declaration countless times throughout my life.

All because of *The Elephant Man* and the power of story.

A week before my family left Los Angeles to move back to our home state of Georgia, we celebrated our daughter's graduation from preschool.

It was a perfect Southern California day. Outside a whimsical cottage-turned-school in West Hollywood, children played, and adults enjoyed lunch from food trucks.

I was sitting on the steps eating a hamburger when a man sat beside me. His pants and work boots were speckled with dried paint. Peripherally, I could tell he had a thick and enviable flock of gray, wavy hair.

I knew immediately who it was. *David Lynch.*

He was also eating a burger. We exchanged nods.

"I'm David, Lula's dad," he said. "I'm Michael—Asher, and Georgia's dad," I replied.

We finished our burgers, and as "un-Hollywood" and as organic as I could make it, I seized the moment.

"I have to tell you something, David. The Elephant Man changed my life."

His eyes lit up.

I continued: "I learned more about grace from your film than I ever did from a church pulpit."

I did not expect what happened next. David punched me in the arm and declared, "F&!% yeah!" And then we had an awesome, heartfelt conversation about *The Elephant Man*.

I watched this film as a child. It never left me.

Decades later, I had the opportunity to look the man who made this film in the eye and explain to him that something he invested years of *his life* making . . . changed *my life.*

It was an unexpected blessing and, once again, a powerful testimony to how stories can change lives.

It was a full-circle gift that brought artful closure to our chapter in Los Angeles.

Always be aware of gifts that open and close the chapters of your life . . . they are everywhere on your road to Ithaka.

WISE AS YOU WILL HAVE BECOME

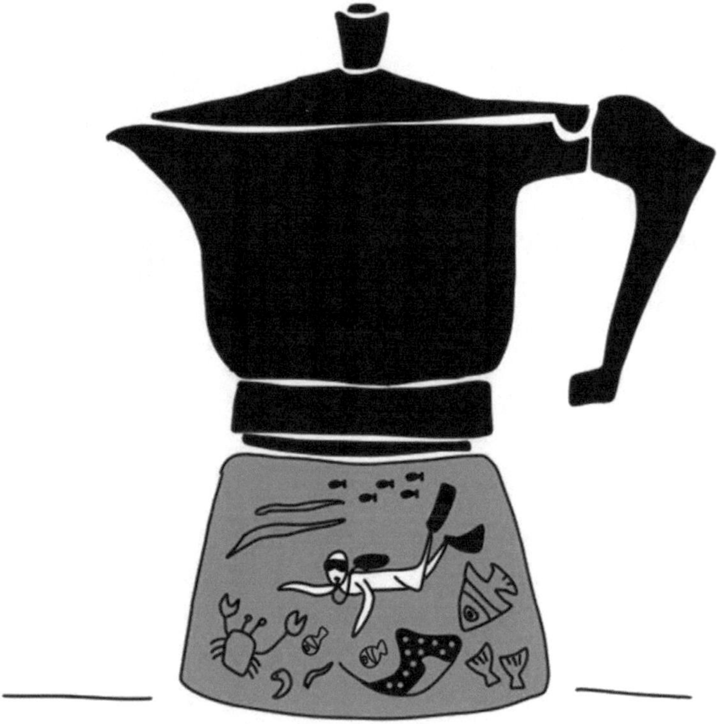

FRESHLY GROUND

On an oppressively sweltering day in August 2003, New York City experienced one of its worst blackouts in modern history.

I was living on Hudson Street in the West Village in an apartment I moved into after 9/11 forced a mass exodus from the city. I was months away from proposing to my then-girlfriend, now wife. I was running the concierge department for two hotels in Tribeca, just ten blocks from Ground Zero.

To the best of my ability, I was laying a foundation for my future—to be married, employed, and poised to pursue our creative lives together in the romance of the West Village, which, in my opinion, was and still is the best neighborhood in the United States.

On the morning of the blackout, I suffered a first-world panic.

How am I going to make coffee?!

So, I ventured into the neighborhood to explore the fallout from the blackout.

That particular walk led me to a brand-new coffee shop on West 10th Street, which had just opened a few blocks away.

And when I say brand new, I mean brand new. It opened the very morning of the blackout.

Jack's Stir Brew was New York City's first fully organic, fair trade, shade-grown coffee shop.

That day, I found my new home away from home and made a lifelong friend.

Jack Mazzola, the charming proprietor and namesake, was on the sidewalk, surrounded by quiet hope and the loud hum of a compressor he had borrowed from his father's auto body shop to generate power for his patented stir-brew coffee machine.

A crowd of cranky, balmy locals sought anything to give them a sense of normalcy. Coffee, the great peacemaker, was the common ground that provided uncommon characters with a much-needed community.

After all, Jack's was the only business operating during the forty-eight-hour blackout. But it was *never* business as usual with Jack.

He gave coffee away for free during the blackout, earning loyal customers and friendships. Years later, this tiny brick-and-wood shop with only four tables and a few counter spots was established as "New York City's Best Coffee," according to New York Magazine.

New Jersey-born and bred, Jack overflowed with passion, intellectual curiosity, and entrepreneurial spirit.

He invented a patented coffee machine that, for the next eighteen years, would help create a new coffee culture and change the cafe experience in New York City, stretching beyond Manhattan into Long Island's Amagansett and Montauk.

He was the life force and energy in his shops, treating every customer the same—from Italian octogenarian and our dear friend Joe Colombo to actors like Daniel Day-Lewis.

There was no hierarchy at Jack's.

All were welcomed, and everyone belonged.

There was a sense of place rooted in the golden age of human connection and conversation before smartphones forever altered social dynamics. It was a true "third space" where I spent time writing, reading, and engaging with friends, family, and visitors, all over stir-brewed coffee.

This formula of creativity and humility catalyzed unexpected growth. Jack went on to open eight more shops. His accolades and attention garnered interest from Starbucks' Howard Schultz and many others. He fielded offers to acquire the company. Jack was even a question on *Jeopardy*.

But money, fame, or fortune never drove his heart.

He was galvanized by the human experience, the inexplicable magic of creating community, and the wealth of authentic connection.

Jack created something extraordinary.

But it doesn't end there.

This American dream turned into his nightmare.

After opening his final coffee shop at the multi-billion-dollar development Hudson Yards, Jack's business suffered from crippling interest rates and untenable construction overages.

Eighteen years after that auspicious opening day during the blackout, Jack would turn over his entire company to creditors.

He lost it all—his name, brand, patent, income, and hope.

Decades of blood, sweat, and tears that were woven into his dreams harvested a painful loss he barely survived.

Jack and his girlfriend broke up.

And then the pandemic arrived and almost took him out.

Here is the hard truth: **life will grind us down**.

But that doesn't mean something beautiful won't come from the grind.

When coffee beans are ground into a fine powder and hot water is pressed into them, carbon dioxide is released, creating crema, the thick, delicious cream and aromatic beginning of all espresso drinks.

This crema can only be made by grinding beans followed by intense pressure.

When we are ground down, something fresh, beautiful, and new can often and only then be created.

The rich aroma of our lives results from the intense pressure of our circumstances.

I will forever be grateful for what Jack created and the countless moments and cups of coffee I enjoyed at the original shop on 10th Street.

Today, Jack has discovered a renewed purpose.

While the world was suffocating, he found a new landscape of beauty and peace underwater. When the profound loss of his identity as Jack took his breath away, Jack discovered new breath and life, reinventing himself as a scuba diver and certified instructor and traveling the world above and below the water's surface.

He has redirected his passion, curiosity, and entrepreneurial spirit into a dimension he would have never discovered if he had not been completely ground down.

Jack's identity and purpose were not limited to the four walls of a coffee shop.

There is freedom outside, and sometimes, we rise up by first going deeper down.

Jack is not where he thought he would be.
But he is exactly where he is supposed to be.

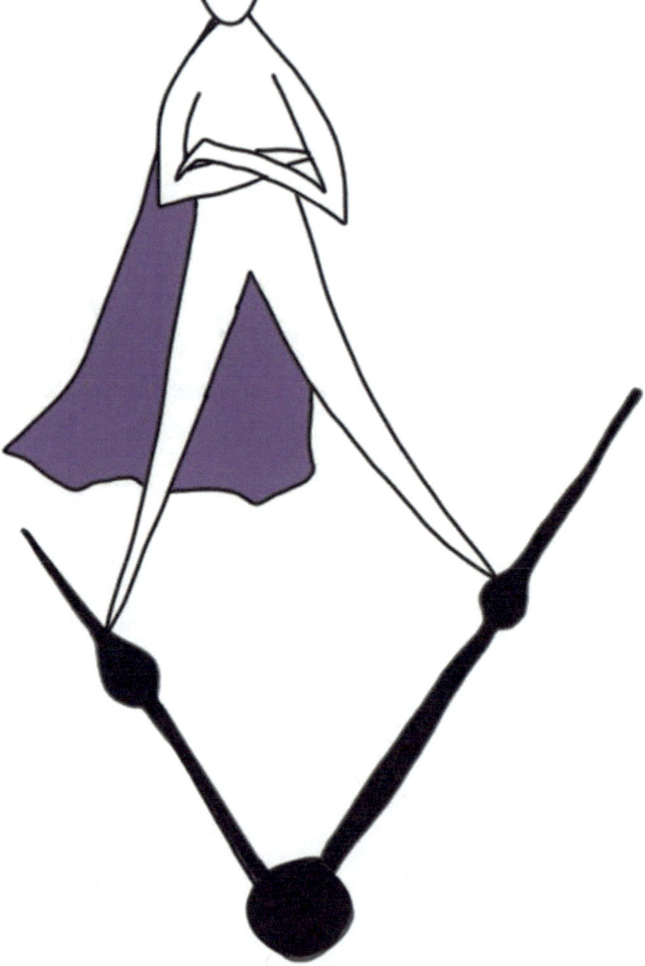

TIME

While living in Los Angeles, my wife and I had this guiding principle in our house:

Things of quality have no fear of time.

I print this phrase, tuck it in books and jacket pockets, and plaster it on the cover of my journals.

It is a reminder that what is truly valuable and of the highest quality will always remain relevant and appreciated over time... *without fear.*

The twenty-four-hour news cycle runs on fear. It's the fuel poured on the fire that culture stokes. Everywhere we turn, there is something to shake our stability, inflame our anxieties, and create unrest in our souls.

The fear of the unknown.

FOMO.

The fear of losing.

The fear of losing it all.

The fear of running out.

The fear of running out of time.

On our journey to Ithaka, it is crucial to remember timeless things of quality. Our dreams, talents, and passions. Our ethics, morals, and values. Our faiths and beliefs. Our integrity and convictions. Our closest relationships.

We may have limited time on earth, but we do not need to fear time. It can be our friend, work in our favor, and be spent on the things of quality that fear can never take away.

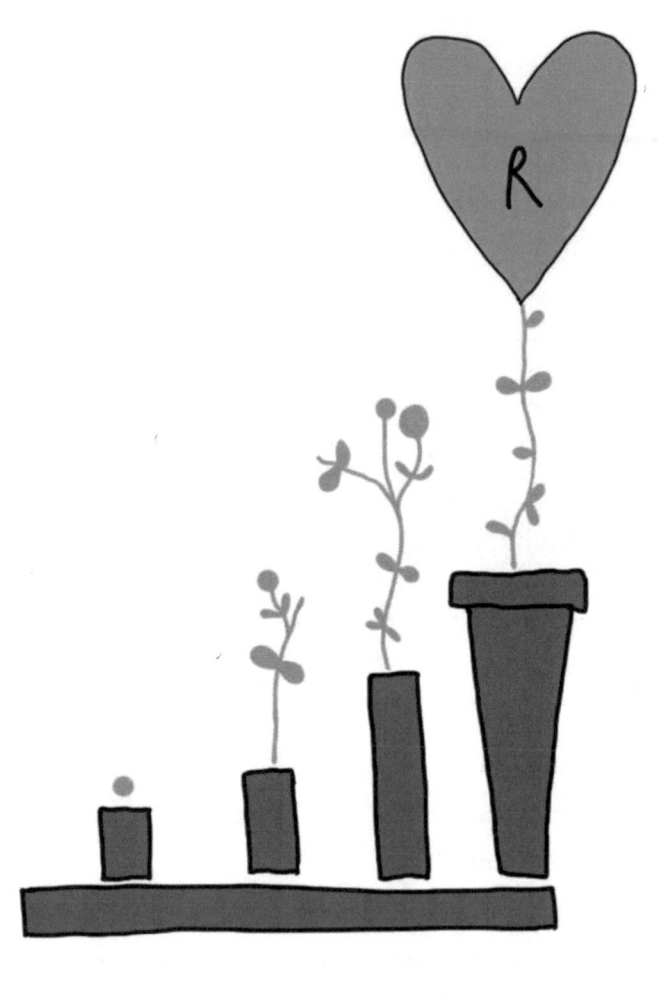

INTENTION
→

ROI

Return on investment (ROI) is a financial metric used to evaluate the profitability of an investment. ROI is calculated by dividing the gain from an investment by its cost.

Let's say you purchase a home you intend to rent.

The purchase cost is $300,000, and you spend $50,000 on repairs for a total investment of $350,000. Over the next year, you collect $40,000 in rental income and pay $15,000 in property taxes, insurance, and maintenance.

$40,000 (net profit) - $15,000 (expenses) = $25,000

$25,000 (net profit)/$350,000 (cost of investment) = .071 or 7.1%

In this scenario, you would make a 7.1% return on your investment.

However, no investment comes with a guaranteed return.

Especially dreams.

The reality is that our dreams have more costs than guarantees.

But what if we flipped the script and defined another kind of ROI?

RETURN ON INTENTION

What if the flowers of our flourishing started with the seeds of our intention?

What beauty would blossom in our lives, families, and communities?

We invest time, energy, preparation, sweat, tears, and prayers, but it is impossible to translate these investments onto a spreadsheet.

I moved to New York City out of high school to pursue a life as a storyteller. Initially, I wanted to be an actor, but my intentions eventually evolved into writing. I landed a survival job, began taking acting classes, developed my craft, and started the long, arduous process of auditioning for paid creative work.

Before technology transformed how we live, I would get a weekly trade paper called *Backstage* and scour it for opportunities. Short films, NYC student thesis films, plays, musicals, industrials, commercials, background work, etc.

I went in for all of it. I landed an agent and formalized the audition process. Email and Internet did not exist back then, so I would go to the agent's office, read the script, and remove the scenes for the audition called "sides."

I cannot begin calculating the hours, years, and decades invested in such uncertain pursuits.

Yet, I can tell you that my intentions have always stayed the same. Since entering my high school drama department, I have intended to tell stories with like-minded, like-hearted collaborators and create work that generates value for others.

From theater to film, children's books to poetry, business, and charity, the return of my intention has been rewarding.

While difficult to calculate or quantify an exact percentage, when we invest, especially when we invest in serving others, the returns can be exponential.

What are the returns on **your** intentions?

A FEW GOOD PEOPLE

You don't need everyone to love you…
just a few good people.
—Charity Barnum, The Greatest Showman

I love the film *The Greatest Showman*. We have watched this film countless times with our two daughters. It chronicles the rise and fall of P.T. Barnum and how his pursuit for worldwide fame almost tore his family apart.

The film resonates with me creatively and personally.

It celebrates music, theater, misfits, and, most importantly, family. It is the hero's journey as a showman, the exploration of the human condition set in the sordid world of the circus, and how the insatiable pursuit of **more** humbly leads back to a place of **enough**.

Last night, we watched it again, and something connected with me in a way that it had not previously. Barnum and his wife, Charity, are in their bedroom as he packs for a nationwide tour with the Swedish sensation Jenny Lind. Charity implores her husband to stay. He says he *must* go for his daughters.

"Look around you; they have everything," she replies. "When will it ever be enough for you?"

Phineas explains how his father was treated like dirt and how he was treated like dirt, and that his children would not be.

Then Charity said something that gut-punched me.

"You don't need everyone to love you . . . just a few good people."

When we talk about quality over quantity—this is it.

A few good people vs. everyone.

The power of a few good, loyal and loving people embarking on the journey with us no matter where it leads cannot be underestimated or under appreciated.

These relationships are worth more than any fortune we could ever chase.

Who are *your* **few good people**?

For *whom* are *you* one of the **few good people**?

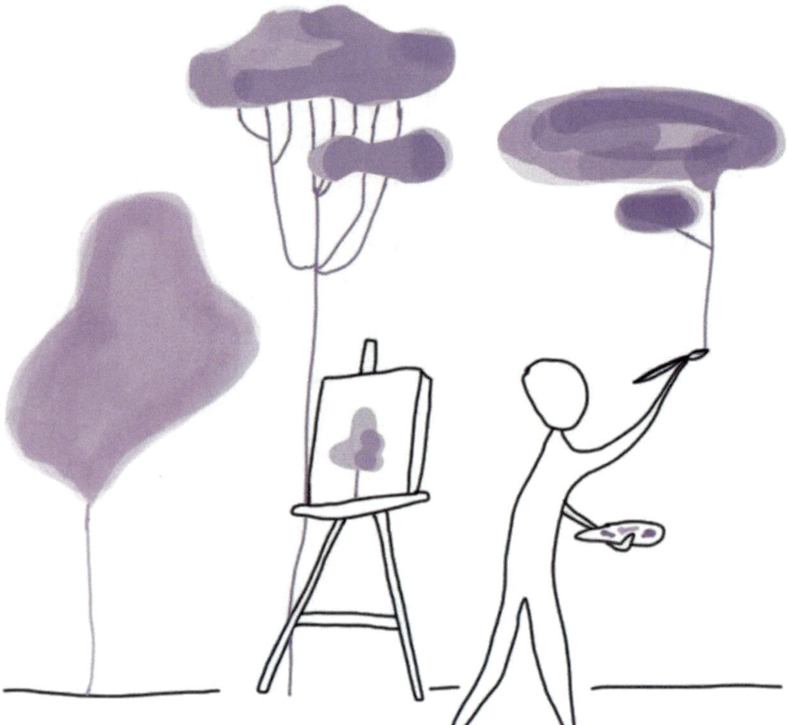

ENVIRONMENT

*The creative process is heavily influenced
by the environment we choose to create in.*
—Salvador Dali

John Klymshyn is an author, a coach, a speaker, and my good friend. Over the years, he has sent me photos of his workspace from different homes, cities, and offices—the meticulously crafted custom-built guitar on his wall. The view from his office window after Idaho's first snow. The pithy quotes and original sayings scribbled on note cards and ordered on his desk.

Sometimes, our conversations are about the environments we intentionally create for ourselves and what is working—or not. Once, John noted he was feeling creatively stunted. I suggested he declutter his space. He took it to heart, sending me photos of a freshly de-congested office. It looked like a space where he could get to work and be inspired.

Our environment can ignite—or stifle—our best work and imagination. The ambiance we engineer in our homes and offices shapes our creative output and stimulates an atmosphere charged with possibility. It is one of the reasons coffee shops have such a magnetic appeal.

On our journey in life, we will find ourselves in many environments: homes, schools, churches, offices, cubicles, labs, parks, public and private spaces, work and rest places, not to mention perhaps the most inspiring of all—the actual environment—the natural wonder of the great outdoors.

We must be intentional about the environments we create and place ourselves in. It's possible that *what* you create may be an environment *where* you create something beyond what you ever thought possible.

My office is small and doubles as a guest room.

The room is filled with books, art, and plants (imperatives to a well-appointed space, according to my mother-in-law).

The bookshelves house the books that inspire me the most. Music usually plays from the Amazon Dot hidden behind a framed photo of Bob Dylan.

It is my sanctuary for curiosity and creativity.

It is a sacred place where I pray, write, work, and have meaningful conversations with family and friends.

I feel hopeful in the space I created to create in.

But it is also a space where I wrestle with frequent discouragement and grapple with many funks and failures.

These spaces we create are the exterior representations of our interior landscapes.

It is the physical matter of what matters most.

To care for our creativity, we must care for our environment.

EVERY DAY YOU GET OLDER —THAT'S THE LAW

When we first meet The Sundance Kid, he faces off with John Macon, the rugged proprietor of Macon's Saloon. The Sundance Kid has been accused of cheating after wiping out every player, including Macon.

Insulted, he has been asked to leave the saloon—*without* his winnings. Macon is standing now, his itchy trigger finger inches from his gun, ready to draw it if things get unruly.

The Sundance Kid is still slumped in his seat, defiant if not sad.

Enter Butch Cassidy, a non-violent gang leader who uses words, charm, and good looks to maneuver them out of hairy situations, including this one.

Macon says to Butch, "You with him, get yourselves out of here."

Butch knows his partner. He knows he will refuse to leave the premises. So, he drops down beside Sundance to persuade him to leave. "I wasn't cheating," the Kid says multiple times.

As the scene escalates, so do Butch's attempts to get them out of there without a bullet to the chest. He tells Sundance that Macon is ready, his hand near his gun. He doesn't know how fast he is, and he doesn't look like he intends to lose.

Butch explains, "Well, I'm over the hill—it can happen to you—every day you get older—that's the law."

We will stop here to give credit to William Goldman, who created these memorable characters in *Butch Cassidy and The Sundance Kid*.

After recently re-watching the film, that bit of dialogue hit home.

The line was spoken in 1969 by Paul Newman, our beloved Butch Cassidy.

Here we are, over five decades later, and Paul Newman is gone, yet his character's line resonates.

Robert Redford is still here.

The Sundance Kid, at eighty-eight years old, refuses to leave the premises.

Today is all you've got.

Double down on it.

You have the cards you've been dealt.

So, play your hand well.

Butch won't be there to help you.

Nobody leaves the saloon alive.

DULCE FAR NIENTE
(The sweetness of doing nothing)

Being of Italian heritage, I often have wondered why it is so difficult for me to sit still.

To just be. To do nothing.

My way of life was slower when I traveled to Italy and other Mediterranean countries.

It seemed like most people were so good at doing nothing and sitting at cafes, sipping coffee, conversing, playing chess, reading, staring into the great unknown, etc.

It's mesmerizing to step out of your environment and experience a different culture, a new way of life, and a new perspective.

Years ago, I was at a grocery store in Kolonaki, a hip neighborhood in Athens, Greece. The clerk sat on a stool, casually scanning my groceries with one hand while holding a cigarette in another. She had a mug of fresh coffee next to the register. She didn't have a care in the world (I love the Greeks!). Yes, she was doing something, but she was doing something with the sweetness of doing nothing.

Our culture is obsessed with being busy.

I've noticed how often I have asked somebody, "How are you doing?"

The answer usually is some variation of busy.

I'm swamped. I've been so crazy lately. You know, busy.

It's a badge of honor to tell others how busy we are. Sometimes, I follow up the "how are you" question with, "Busy doing what?"

I ask myself this question frequently.

What am I doing that makes me so busy?

Is it just busy work, or is there a higher purpose in generating value for others in the work in which I am investing my time and energy?

I am sure you have heard of *The Parable of the Mexican Fisherman*. It is unclear where the parable originated. I first encountered it in Tim Ferris's The Four-Hour Work Week.

But it goes something like this:

At a small coastal Mexican village, an American investment banker stood at the pier, observing a lone fisherman dock his small boat carrying several large yellowfin tunas. Impressed by the fish's quality, the banker struck up a conversation.

"How long did it take you to catch those?" asked the banker, intrigued.

The fisherman replied with a smile, "Just a little while."

Perplexed, the banker questioned, "Why don't you stay out longer and catch more fish?"

The fisherman explained, "I have enough to support my family's immediate needs."

Curiosity got the better of the banker, who probed further, "but what do you do with the rest of your time?"

The fisherman replied, "I sleep in, fish a little, play with my children, take siestas with my wife, and in the evenings, I stroll into the village to sip wine and play guitar with my friends."

The banker chuckled dismissively and said, "I am an accomplished Harvard MBA, and I can help you. You should spend more time fishing and sell the extra catch. With the profits, you can buy a bigger boat, and eventually, you'll have a fleet of boats. Instead of selling to middlemen, you can sell directly to the processor. In time, you can open your own cannery and control the entire supply chain. You'll need to leave this village and move to a big city like Mexico City, Los Angeles, and ultimately, New York City to expand your business."

The fisherman pondered for a moment and asked, "But how long will all this take?"

The banker replied, "It will probably take around fifteen to twenty years."

The fisherman then inquired, "And what will happen after that?"

The banker grinned, "That's the best part. Once your company goes public with an IPO, you'll become very rich. You can make millions!"

The fisherman contemplated the banker's words and asked, "Millions? And then what?"

The banker, slightly taken aback, replied, "Well, then you can retire. You can move to a small coastal fishing village, sleep late, fish a little, play with your children, take siestas with your wife, and in the evenings, stroll into the village to sip wine and play guitar with your friends."

The power of story.

Old words become new again.

After living in cities like New York, Los Angeles, Chicago, and Auckland, the need to be and constantly do something at all times is built into the "production narrative."

We must be producing *something* at all times. *Must we?*

I have become friends with a charming Italian restaurateur over the years. He is a force of energy; everyone loves him, and his love for what he does is reflected in every touch-point of his newest restaurant. It is a place to meet friends and family for a coffee or an incredible meal.

The music is excellent.

The atmosphere is buzzing.

The arts are celebrated.

The community is loyal.

He created something special.

But at the time of this writing, he is lying in a hospital bed recovering from a massive heart attack, and his road to recovery right now is as long as it is uncertain.

It's a cautionary tale. To be very clear, I am not criticizing him. I, too, have worked through overbearing stress to keep a business afloat, and several times, I thought it would take me out.

We are in hot pursuit of our Ithakas. We think that when we get *there*, we will undoubtedly possess what we have been chasing all of these uncertain years. And then we can finally do nothing. For some, doing nothing is far from sweet. My father's retirement was terrible for him and not at all what he thought it would be. Here are other examples from people I know:

_____ dedicated his entire life to his career, working long hours and sacrificing personal relationships and hobbies with the hope of retiring comfortably. Unfortunately, a few years before his planned retirement, he was diagnosed with a severe illness that limited his ability to enjoy his retirement years fully.

_____ was driven and ambitious, pouring all her time and energy into building her career. She consistently prioritized work over relationships, believing she would have plenty of time to nurture them later in life. She missed family gatherings, neglected friendships, and rarely made time for romantic relationships. As the years went by, she achieved professional success but gradually realized the toll her choices had taken on her personal life. She found herself isolated and disconnected from loved ones. Once strong relationships had weakened, and some had even faded away.

I do not have all the answers. I can only seek the answers to the questions that pertain to my life.

I do know that the pandemic was a turning point.

In December 2019, I was starting to fall apart.

Work was overwhelming.

We had moved twice in one year, once cross-country and then the second time within our neighborhood.

I was in Las Vegas one week, New York City the next, and Ireland a few weeks later.

I would wake up each morning and begin my day in bed, stressed, reading and reacting to fifty to seventy emails.

I was burnt out.

My body felt broken; my mental health was shaky.

Yet, 2018-2019 were the most successful years—in business and on paper—I have ever had.

A few short months later, when the world was forced to stay home, work ceased, the tyranny of my inbox disappeared, the anxiety of not doing enough vanished, and I finally, wholeheartedly, unabashedly, did nothing.

Despite global uncertainty and local unpredictability, *dulce far niente* was a reality.

The air was different.

The sounds in the air were more pleasant.

I could hear birdsong more clearly as they were not competing with planes overhead or rushed vehicles on the road.

I slept (well, a little better).

I took long walks with my wife.

I played more with my children.

I threw a baseball around with my neighbors.

I discovered basketball (see "They're Aggressive").

I read books I wanted to read.

I created things I wanted to make.

There were absolutely no expectations.

Yes, I did some things.

But they were done with the spirit and sweetness of doing nothing.

The world is back now.

Along with new demands, expectations, and anxieties.

As we continue our journeys to Ithaka, we must make rest stops to discover the sweetness that often comes from doing nothing.

I am happy to report that, as of the publication of this book, my friend is alive and recuperating with his family in Italy.

CREATIVE RESILIENCE

During Covid, I wrote a "children's book for adults," an anxiety-driven and creative response to the pandemic.

It was an ambitious attempt to tackle spirituality and philosophy with just 464 words. Although it looked and felt like a children's book (with whimsical illustrations by the very talented Todd Wilkerson*), it was written for adults.

When I had an early print version of the book, I gave it to my wife, who sat on the couch and read it in five minutes.

She closed the book and kindly stated: **"I don't get it."**

A year of my life went into that little book, and for my life partner and closest critic to not "get it," ... well, I allowed myself to go into a giant funk. But that funk led to me reimagining the book and releasing something I am proud of.

Many people still don't get it, but many do. I could not control the outcome, but my wife's constructive criticism improved my writing.

Several years ago, I produced a staged reading of one of my plays in Los Angeles. It was a personal play loosely based on my family, addiction, and dysfunction. It was an invited audience of 100 people, many of whom were in the industry.

What I envisioned in my head and what was presented on stage that night was worlds apart.

The play was a *flop*. Wow, it was so awkward. You could feel the tension in the air. Uncomfortable energy filled the theatre. Guests escaped before having to lie to my face about what they thought about the play.

I *really* needed resilience in that moment.

I wanted to crawl under a rock and disappear. Hiding and/or sitting in the funk for a while is normal. It is human.

Resilience encourages you out of that space because there is more work to do, more ideas to explore, and more people to serve. The show must go on.

Recently, my wife and I spoke on a panel for The Trilith Foundation, an organization near and dear to our hearts. Their mission is to enrich the lives of creatives who inspire the world and encourage the study and art of human flourishing (see more information at the end of this chapter).

In preparation, I considered what practices I must pursue to make my journey to Ithaka more resilient. I came up with a list that would also make it more *enjoyable*. We sometimes need to remember to have fun and enjoy the process.

1. **Find a meaningful spiritual practice:** My Christian faith is the key to my resilience because I have hope and peace that transcend my creativity, work, and success. God loves me more than I love my dreams, which gives me perspective and peace.
2. **Take the risk.** There is no more significant way to build resilience than to take risks. This requires courage, stepping out of your comfort zone, and discovering the vital relationships between vulnerability and strength, confidence and humility.
3. **Connection:** If you're not connected to your work, nobody else will be. Connection builds resilience. In marriage, friendship, faith, and community. We must stay connected to what matters most and, more importantly, to **whom** matters most.

4. **Release:** We must release expectations and understand the difference between an audience and an outcome. We *create* for one. We *release* the other.
5. **Reprioritize:** Ironically, one of the best ways to build resilience in our creative lives is not to make creativity our top priority. Instead, our mental, physical, and spiritual health must be the priority. Serving our families and friends must be a priority. Serving our communities must be a priority. Our commitments and vows must be a priority. Sometimes, the menial is most meaningful.
6. **You are enough:** It may not feel like this sometimes, but you are. Your voice is unique and has immense value. Remembering and reminding yourself of this builds resilience over time.
   You are enough.
7. **Beauty:** What is beautiful to you? Surround yourself with that beauty. Music, art, poetry, chess, silence, dance, sculptures, paintings, the great outdoors. A simple walk in nature can bring you back to your work with a fresh, restored perspective. Restoration leads to resilience.
8. **Collaboration:** Collaboration elevates your vision by engaging with others who bring dimension and clarity to the work you may have missed. Play rehearsal is my favorite process because actors bring their gifts and interpretations of my words, making them so much better. Collaboration edifies your work with fresh perspectives.
9. **Stop focusing on ourselves:** Artists and creatives are inherently self-centered, egotistical, and operate like the world revolves around them. Sometimes, it's a loud

cry for attention; other times it is a deep quest to fill an empty void. Often, it is necessary hubris. But ultimately there is no fulfillment in filling ourselves with . . . *self.*

10. **Don't buy into the suffering artist myth:** I did and still deal with the consequences of those choices today. Part of being a successful creative is avoiding drama that is not on the stage or the page. There are enough low points in life that you do not to *pursue* hardship to become a compelling creative. Can you create from a place of pain? Yes. Some of my best work was born in a dark place. However, I believe you can best build creative resilience in the light when you operate from well-being and the best version of yourself. This holistic approach includes all areas of our lives: mentally, physically, spiritually, and relationally.

The life of a creative is uncertain and untraditional.

The traditional workforce enjoyed a secure, predictable job at one company for life. My father worked his entire career as a stockbroker (after an early stint as a taxi driver in NYC), and my grandfather worked for Sears Roebuck and Co. for thirty years.

They each received a watch when they "arrived" (retired).

A *timepiece*—a cruel gift if you think about it.

The life of a creative is spent writing stories that may never be read, composing music that may never be heard, and filming, painting, sculpting, and crafting art that may never be seen.

It is a life of doubts and disappointments, profound beauty and bewilderment. One day, we think our work is excellent; the next day, we think it's terrible. The vacillation between self-confidence and self-doubt becomes old and exhausting.

As a creative, you confront three primary sources of critical feedback:

The Work. Yourself. Others.

You will often be your own worst critic.

Sometimes you have to ignore yourself.

Others will always be willing to criticize your work, which is subjective and subject to countless opinions. Sometimes, you have to ignore others, too.

However, you can use criticism to help you grow by first creating an honest framework where criticism optimizes and enhances instead of destroying and demeaning.

Create a trusted, creative board of directors in your life. Three or four people who know and love you and can offer objective, constructive criticism. My wife and a few close friends are on my creative board of directors. Seek advice, feedback, and honesty from your community of truth-tellers in the innermost circles to best serve the outermost circles—the people you will never meet.

As creatives, here are a few questions to ask ourselves once in a while: What are you making? Where are you going to make it? For whom are you making it? When are you going to make it? Finally, **why** are you making it?

The first play I ever wrote (the one previously mentioned Edward Albee encouraged me to write) was about writers and the perils of fame and fortune.

This is one of the lines from the play:

> *"Criticism and praise are both demons.*
> *One has a sweeter voice."*

Sometimes, we must embrace the criticism.

More often, we must ignore the praise.

Choose what voices you listen to.
Work quietly. Work diligently.
Only tell people about what you are making once it is made.
Achievement is not a solution. Success is not a savior.

A very special thanks to: The Town at Trilith, Trilith Studios, The Trilith Foundation, The Trilith Institute, Rob Parker, Dan T. Cathy, Frank Patterson, Elizabeth Dixon, Michelle McConnell, Daniel Bashta, Aaron Fortner, Hannah Webb, Alston Causey, Dr. Tyler Thigpen, Joe Castillo, Huntington Brown, Noray Sanchez, Jordan Preston, Tiffany Harris, Tiffany Summers, Vanessa Siguenza, Krissy Lewis, Phil Brane, Tia Miller, Fred Odom, Jake Pitman, Logynn Ferrall, Kevyn Bashore, Daniel Seith, Al Mead, Ed Johnson, Lydia Grae Barbee, Gwen Brown, Anna Messer, Tiago Magro, Mark & Sharon Fincannon, Carol Williams, Dr. Janice Crenshaw, Dick Piet, Sheryl Rexrode, Natalie McIntyre, Craig Scott, Adam Hart, Josh Lee, Trey Strawn, Blaine Hogan, Ross Cathy, Jeffrey Stepakoff, Marshall Jones, Dr. Jennifer Franklin, Shannon Lake, Matt McClain, Ray Gibson, Mimi Tin, Jody Noland, Wynn Everett, Abby McCollum, and others who work so hard to cast and execute a vision for a community of families, friends, and storytellers. Thank you for investing in the future of creativity and flourishing.

To learn more about The Trilith Foundation and make a donation, please visit: trilithfoundation.org

A portion of the royalties from this book will be donated to The Trilith Foundation's Mental Health Subsidy and other initiatives to help professional creatives.

***

*To enjoy Todd Wilkerson's creative work, please visit: thetoddwilkerson.com

THE MARVELOUS JOURNEY

The two most important days of your life are the day you were born, and the day you find out why.
—**Mark Twain**

There are an estimated tens of thousands of books on the topic of purpose, ranging from self-help, fiction and nonfiction, personal growth, philosophy, and leadership.

Viktor Frankl's *Man's Search for Meaning* is a profound starting point for gaining insight into the search for meaning even during the worst imaginable conditions.

Rick Warren's *The Purpose Driven Life* is the bestselling book of all time next to the Bible.

There are other wonderful nonfiction works exploring purpose through the state of complete immersion and focus, which the late Mihaly Csikszentmihalyi coined as "flow" in his groundbreaking book *Flow*.

The Book of Joy: Lasting Happiness in a Changing World, written by the Dalai Lama, Desmond Tutu, and Douglas Carlton Abrams, offers a spiritual approach to finding purpose and lasting happiness by serving others.

Fictionally, *The Alchemist* is an allegorical fable about a young shepherd who embarks on a journey to Egypt to find the treasure of his dreams. It is a story about following your heart, taking risks, and finding your true purpose in life.

Pablo Picasso once said, "The meaning of life is to find your gift. The purpose of your life is to give it away."

What would the world look like if we discovered our gift only then to give it away to bless and serve others?

Discovering the purpose of our life may take a lifetime.

Purpose can change with circumstances.

Sometimes, the seasons of our lives are multi-purposed.

In this season of life, *my* purpose is to be a husband, father, and friend.

And tell stories (and, yes, when I can, play basketball).

Simon Sinek's work explores why better than anyone.

He wrote the internationally bestselling book *Start with Why*, inspiring leaders and readers worldwide to discover the underlying purpose of their lives and work.

Before Simon Sinek, there was Constantine Cavafy and his ancient poem about our modern journey to Ithaka.

This journey *is* marvelous.

Our journey is our **why**.

It is our **reward**.

Without it, we would never have set out.

You were born for this marvelous journey. So . . .

Whatever your dream destination is,

wherever you are on your marvelous journey,

you may not be where you thought you would be.

You may not have arrived.

You may feel lost.

You may have lost hope.

But take heart . . .

You are exactly where you are supposed to be.

Keep going!

Ithaka awaits.

Only those who risk going too far
can possibly find out how far one can go.
—T.S. Eliot

ACKNOWLEDGEMENTS

Working tirelessly in uncertainty… alone… dreaming… for hours or decades… creating something out of nothing… this often feels like a solo endeavor.

Nothing comes into the world without a loving community's unwavering support and encouragement.

On our journey to Ithaka, some people will model, inspire, challenge, sharpen, and engage with us in many ways that have nothing to do with the art and everything to do with the artist.

It is impossible to quantify.

Sometimes, these people are in our lives for a reason, a season, or forever.

This may be the only book I attempt to get away with such a ridiculously long list of people.

I can't help it.

I have many people to thank, and each deserves acknowledgment.

It is an embarrassment of riches to have so many people from so many places and chapters of my life.

Forgive me if you were not mentioned by name.

You know who you are and how you bless my life. These individuals have influenced, encouraged, modeled, challenged, inspired, engaged, and sharpened me on my journey to Ithaka. They are the wealth I have gained so far along the way.

I am a better human being, artist, and citizen of the world because of the following people:

My Dear Mother: You are the sweetest mom ever! You have always supported and encouraged me. From a young age, you taught me the importance of reading, expressing gratitude, faith, appreciating art, and caring for each other, for nature, and, of course, for animals. You are an incredible artist and a beloved mother, mother-in-law, Grandmom, and friend. Thank you for your love and support. I love you so much, Mom!

My lovely sisters, **Allison Albanese, Valerie Albanese, Stacy Dumont** (+ **Bob, Robert, Ellie, and Noey**), and **Anthony Crane**: Each of you has always been so loving and encouraging. I am inspired by your unique, creative contributions to the world through food, travel, photography, theatre, music, and writing. Thank you for your unwavering, loving support. I am so grateful for our small, prayerful, and mighty family.

Ed and Avis Everett: The very best in-laws in the world. Your prayers, encouragement, and generosity are more than a daughter, son-in-law, or granddaughter could ever ask for, expect, or imagine. Thank you for being my second set of parents. I am forever grateful for you both. You are the best Lovie and Pop in the world, and your intellectual curiosity is only matched by your faithfulness. I can't wait for our next meal and adventure—and maybe some good old-fashioned pontificating!

Aunt Vinnie Carpenter and my late **Uncle Larry Carpenter**: From the early days of sleeping on the floor in your living room, if it were not for you (and the loving patience of Grandma Gracie, Steven, and David), I would not have been given the foundation to start my life in New York City. Your hospitality, love, and support will never be forgotten. I love you. Uncle Larry, you will be greatly missed (RIP August 2024).

Uncle Bruce Walz and my late, great **Aunt Renata, Jennifer, Gene, Rachel, Gonzalo,** and **Renata**: Thank you for your lifelong love of family, food, and faith. Your generosity, intellect, and hearts are unmatched. Thank you for making our summers magical and memorable. Some of my best childhood and adult moments were spent with the Walz Family.

Jane Chappell: Aunt Jane, you are a rare, true gem. Thank you for being so kind, generous, and loving to our family. We love you so much!

Steve and Zan Wright: I am so grateful to have you as a second family, along with Stephen & Karen, Randy & Maggie, and all those sweet children. Thank you for your love, generosity, and encouragement!

Craig Archibald: I cannot imagine how many paths we crossed on the streets and places of New York City before you moved in next door to us in Los Angeles. That was a fortunate day, the forging of a lifelong friendship and brotherhood rooted in love, laughter, and art. Your generosity and commitment to storytelling and storytellers (along with your Canadian kindness and Saskatoon suave) are among many reasons you are so beloved. I am so grateful for and to you, my friend and brother. And so are the artists you encourage.

Luis Banuelos: Your talent is exceeded only by your heart. Your spiritual transformation is awe-inspiring, and your musical gifts are poised to explode in ways you cannot imagine. I am grateful for you.

Daniel Bashta: Your heart's too big to wear on your sleeves (besides, those are fully covered. Friendship is poetry, a rhyme and rhythm, with stanzas that give meaning to life's wanderings. You are a soulful, contemplative, thoughtful artist with just enough acerbic wit to keep the light flickering. Thank you for being that friend. We love you and Taylor and are grateful for your friendship. Blessings, brother.

Lothaire Bluteau: "Listen to the music of the line." These were the first words you said to me. For decades after we met in that recording studio in Manhattan, I lost count of the long walks in the village, the coffee and talks, the purity of your insights, and the depth of your honesty. You're the consummate artist and artistic genius in my book.

Anthony Bovino: You originally called this a "map for the mapless." I am grateful to have reconnected days before the world shut down. Our journeys, from New York to Atlanta, have been so interesting. Thank you for your vulnerability and strength. Your humor, sense of design, and loyalty are rare. Keep creating and executing your ideas. I am so encouraged by how you continuously seek to serve and edify all those around you. You make the world a better place, AB.

Thor Benander: Country. I don't even know where to begin with you. You are the smart in smart ass. Even though I still struggle to forgive you for arrogantly showing up late on the first day of acting class, my love for you and our friendship knows no words. My first friend in NYC, you made embarking on this journey so much better, much funnier, and richer. We love you, Juliana and your children.

Dusty Brown: Hey Buddy! From the days of NYC, you are one I confidently call a creative contemporary. Your passion for music, literature, film, and chess endeared me to a long, lyrical friendship. Your faith, talent, grace, and sense of humor abound, making my life so rich. So proud of you, "Sketch," and all that follows! *Come here!*

Jason Burkey: Well, what can I say? A new ware to sell! I am very grateful to know you and your family and am always inspired by your zest for life, contagious optimism, and quest for adventures. You are a talented lad and a blessing as a husband, father, and friend. We love you, Callie and your boys. I look forward to our next mission trip.

Phil Caruso: "I just made pictures I would've liked to see." – Billy Wilder. Phil Caruso could have said this. Or I will rephrase. I just make friends with people I am fortunate enough to meet for a short period who have a significant impact. That's you, my talented friend.

Dean Chalmers: My Jewish-Italian brother from another mother. You have encouraged and admonished me in ways you can't imagine. You helped pioneer the journey with two daughters. I owe you so much of my deep appreciation for coffee, pizza, and *all* things Israel.

Raymond Clark: There would be no *WillieMichaelRay* without you. If loyalty were a picture, it would be of you. A gentleman and renaissance man, you have always put others before yourself. One of my greatest joys is when I can make you laugh. Thank you for being such a kind, generous, and loyal friend. If everyone had a friend like you, the world would be better. We love you and Cheryl and are so grateful for you.

Nick Cokas: *You know what?* I am showing my work! There is not enough room to say what I need to say. Who would have ever thought an enduring friendship and collaborative spirit would be born from the bowels of a Planet Hollywood bathroom in New York City? One of my oldest and dearest friendships. You have been a deep well of love, encouragement, and honesty through the highs and lows. Friendship is art, and you are a master painter. Your faithful friendship helped me return to my faith and sharpen my art. For that, I will forever be grateful. Our epic discussions around art, faith, and relationships continue to sharpen, challenge, and enlighten. Blessings to you, Roxane and Baby Cokas! I love you! *What do you want from me?*

Steve Cox: You are one of a kind and a true friend. You are always yourself, always hysterical, and always a large part of the Marietta memories. You don't even know the definition of pretense because you are who you are and have never pretended otherwise. What a rarity and refreshment. You are also the original baller. I can't wait to play you 1v1 one day. Love to you and Jill, brother.

David and Niki Dalton: We love having you in our lives. You both are authentic, talented, sweet souls who bring love and light everywhere you go. We are grateful for friendships like yours, which are salt of the earth. We look forward to more creativity and conversations.

Jeff Dark: I blame you for discovering my love for the theater. If it were not for your kindness to drive me home from school and stopping to sign up for the fall production, I might have missed that magical moment. I am blessed to have a friendship as fun, deep, and encouraging as ours. You are a friend, husband, and father whose work ethic, perspective, and creativity have always inspired me. I miss our epic conversations when we lived thousands of miles apart. Blessings on you, Nancy, Sarah & Charlie. *Never underestimate Georgia!*

ZD: Bro. You know what you've meant to me over the years. Thank you for everything. Words cannot justly express my appreciation, love, and respect. Blessings to you and your family always. Grazie mille!

Charlie Drozdyk: You have been part of my life and journey from my very formative years in NYC. You are truly one of a kind. You are smart, funny, with ferocious honesty and fearlessness to be yourself. Your ability to take risks, be entrepreneurial and artistic, and not care about what anyone thinks is beautifully rare. I just wish I saw you more often. I hope wherever you are right now, you are well and thriving.

Keegan Dum: You are one of the nicest (and smartest human beings I've ever met. You are a great husband, dad, and friend. It's been a blessing getting to know you, Carina, and your children over the years, and we appreciate having such salt-of-the-earth family friends.

Matthew Goodwin: You and Mandi were our first real friends when we moved back to Georgia. Your story is beautiful. Your marriage, all of your sons, and creativity are sources of inspiration, love and resilience. We love you and are so grateful to have you in our lives and hearts.

Adam Epstein: Heartbreakingly, you passed away right before this was published. From the first day of rehearsal for "Cry Baby" to deep conversations, your creative, theatrical, and intellectual prowess always inspired. Our civil discourse on faith, religion, and politics was consistently elevated and educated. I was grateful to have you in my life. You will be greatly missed, Adam. Shalom, my friend.

Willie Duncan: You are my oldest standing friend. I honestly cannot believe we met in third grade during recess. Few people have the blessing and luxury of calling a friend as old and dear as you. Building a lifelong friendship with you is incredibly rare. In addition, you are a wonderful father and husband and faithful friend to all. Thank you for your love, best friendship, and huge heart. Your kindness and optimism are unmatched and have always amazed me. I am so grateful for you, Gina, Steven, Julia and Michael. I love you!

CF: Thank you for being one of the most authentic people I have ever known. You have given me the generosity of opportunity and experiences I will never forget and will always cherish. Thank you for your support, kindness and challenges over the years.

Matt Geipel: I have enjoyed my many conversations with you and Mela over the years. Thank you for sharing your faith, challenges, and victories. You are good neighbors, friends, and, most importantly, parents. I love hooping with one of your children and enjoy watching another begin her journey to success and adulthood.

Bradley Hasemeyer: Our families' journeys have overlapped in three cities during different times and seasons. You, Keirsten, and your children have been out to sea for a long time, and now to have you landlocked for many years to come is especially heartwarming. We love you both and wish blessing on all your creative endeavors.

Bob Hawk: You are my longtime mentor and oldest friend (in years and to some extent duration). Your love, support, and passion for theatrical and cinematic storytelling and storytellers are unmatched in this world. And so is your heart. Thank you for decades of encouragement. I will always remember the snowstorm in Berlin, our six-hour meals, and our conversations in New York and Los Angeles. You are a national treasure to filmmakers and storytellers everywhere.

Christopher J. Hanke: From the first day of rehearsal, I knew we would be friends. You are Nathan Detroit, Riff, Puck, Henry Higgins, Mark Cohen and Billy Flynn rolled up in one. But you are the best playing Christopher: talented, funny, sincere, faithful, passionate, loyal, and entrepreneurial. So grateful you and Geoffrey are in our lives.

Blaine Hogan: Blaine from Blaine, fellow girl dad, artist, and theatrical misfit wanderer. I am so happy our paths have crossed. Our friendship is one that went deep early on by first reading your book and your story. I look forward to the great things you and Margaret create for the world. And ... I hope you get to play Hamlet one day.

James Jennings: Well, I declare. You are a strapping, firefighting, carpentering troubadour. This isn't Hemingway, Fitzgerald, or Pound. But here we are. Or are we? I had to write to avoid reading. Though time and distance separate, you are a brother and contemporary as close to my heart as ever. NYC memories are nothing without you.

Dom Kegel: I love you, man. What a good, loving husband, father and friend. Such a heart of gold, a terrific athlete, an inspiration on and off the court. Not a false bone in your body. We love your family and are so grateful that you, Susan, and Finland are in our lives.

Tyler Kelley: What a friend, father, and adventurer. You are a confidant, counselor, and comrade. I am so grateful you came into my life. Thank you for your friendship and wisdom that appeals to my left brain. Your recent convictions and decisions will serve you and your little ladies well. And one day, we'll go on an adventure together.

Russ and Kara Kiefer: Build it, and they will come! I'm so proud of you both for dreaming and then doing. You created something special and meaningful, and it's been a real blessing to become friends with you both over these years. You are so generous to this community. Whether it's a pot of soup when somebody is sick or hosting events to help charitable causes, your hearts are golden.

Mary Lynn and Hugh Kirby: We are blessed to have met the loveliest and kindest people when we moved back to Georgia. Your journey has been anything but smooth, but seeing how you have co-captained your life together is inspiring, unique, and beautiful. Just like our sunsets. We wish you and your family continued love, grace and blessings!

Sean Kirkland: You were one of the original misfits I described finding in drama class in high school. Who would have thought that would have led to becoming roommates in NYC, adventures through faith, music, and family, and now seeing you thrive as a therapist, lending your experience and story to serve and help others heal? Much love to Laura (another amazingly talented artist) and your children.

John Klymshyn: *Buon Giorno!* You taught me how to identify, embrace, and appreciate resonance all around us (especially in music, film, and writing. Your skills as an expert communicator and writer, as well as your sense of humor and honesty, continue to inspire. You uprooted your life to make a new one in Idaho, and it's been wonderful to see your "imagination put to work." Let's keep moving our conversations forward.

Tad Lumpkin: Very few men I know have been as committed and consistent in their values and convictions as you. You are willing to risk, move, and reinvent while staying true to your growing family, faith, and purpose. Thank you for your friendship, prayers, and encouragement. God bless you, Berkeley, your boys, and little girl! Love you, brother!

Derek McKee: You add magic to my life. Your humility, kindness, and generosity are not illusions. You are an authentic, old soul who brings magic to the world, especially to the children and communities you graciously serve. And if you read anything in this book, make sure it's the part about Bob Dylan. Keep on keepin' on.

Jack Mazzola: You are the closest I have to an actual brother. My heart is fuller because you're in it. If we could bottle up and share your passion, authenticity, and enthusiasm, the world would feel like one of your coffee shops—brimming with love, community, and creativity. You are one of the greatest gifts New York gave me. Many blessings to come, brother.

Michael McGruther: Neither of us could have written the wild tale of our friendship. Chapters of early days in NYC, special morning orange juice on West 14th, late night shifts at Trattoria Del 'Arte, traversing the dark roads of Hollywood, and the light-filled paths of faith and family have been a blessing. Your wit, talent, and tenacity always encourage. But what inspires me most is your unwavering commitment and passionate voice championing the power of independent storytellers. Love to Michelle and Reagan. Can't wait to see what you create next.

Nate Michaux: You have been a beloved main character in so many of my chapters from New York to Los Angeles; sometimes the herald, other times the shapeshifter, but always the ally. Right now, you are in the dark night of the soul. You will be on the other side of this, in the light. You are crushed, but your heart will prevail. You have so much to offer. Keep your hope, heart, and wit alive, my friend. You are loved by many. And if you ever need a laugh, we will always have... Doma.

Steven MacGeachy: You are a good man, a good man indeed. From boss to colleague to friend, you have been a great source of support, encouragement, and honesty. I have thoroughly enjoyed our many talks over the many years and hope we can work on that project together in the near future! I wish your family all the best in the new chapters of life that have yet to be written.

Eugene Ufuk Masat: Wow. A genuine original, incapable of being duplicated. They don't make them like you anymore—one of my oldest, toughest, and tenderest friends. Our laughter, experiences, meals, walks, workouts, chess, and talks together are unmatched and what makes my memories of New York City so vibrant and vital. I cannot imagine Manhattan—or my life—without you in it, Ufuk!

Frank Muscarello: Although we have not met physically, I appreciate what you've done for me. It has been a genuine pleasure building a friendship and working relationship with you over the years. You are a good man and patriot. I look forward to more of our conversations.

Grant Nieporte: Many years ago, you gave us great encouragement and love with a personal challenge. Your story, family, and career are rooted in everything that matters most. Your dedication to craft, art, and storytelling continues to inspire. Thank you for your honesty and encouragement throughout the years. I hope we can collaborate on something soon. Blessings to you, Jill and your children. Love you!

GN: I have had the unique experience of experiencing some of your most important milestones, challenges, and victories. You have taught me so much. Your faith, integrity, and commitment to growing into a better version of yourself have always inspired me.

Jody Noland: You have been such a treasure to our family, a mentor to our daughters, and an inspiration to our community. Your generosity, thoughtfulness, and uniquely creative way to connect people to who and what matters most is beautiful. Thank you for being you and modeling motherhood, friendship, and mentorship so gracefully.

Guy Nattiv: A beautiful husband, father and artist. Your passion is evident in everything you do. From film to justice to friendship, you and Jaime embody inspiration, passion and storytelling. We are grateful for you both.
Shervin Oskouei: You are one of my oldest, dearest, and smartest friends. You have never let your work ethic and success replace or compromise that giant heart of yours. You are an amazing husband and father (not to mention surgeon and pilot. I am grateful for such a loyal, true friend.
Carol Owens: Who would have thought a unique friendship would have formed when you attended that writers conference in NYC? You have been a prayerful friend, always faithful, vulnerable, and with that acerbic sense of humor. Keep writing and dreaming!
Chris Patton: You're a big guy. Not just physically (I'm happy I have not had to guard you yet in the paint!) but big in heart, in love, in intention, and in serving communities. We are blessed to know you and Jenny!

David Rocksavage: You are one of the kindest, gentlest and creative souls I have ever met. Thank you for being such a generous filmmaker and friend (your wedding gift to us will never be forgotten). Blessings on your family.

Tony Hale: Brother. Talk about a journey. Yours has taken you high and low, East and West, near and far, but you always brought Tony with you, which meant wherever you were, the world was brighter and blessed. We love you and Martel and are excited for your new chapter of life. Much love!
Jon Schaeffer: My fellow girl dad, I don't know if I have ever known anybody quite like you. It's like you are this passionate, compassionate, stylish intellect with a humble heart of gold bursting with love. Your commitment to family and friends (and surfing) inspires! Love you, man!
Simone Scigliano: *Ciao, Simone!* You and Alena are some of the sweetest people we know. Such good, pure hearts. We are happy you moved here and found a new community where you and your family can thrive, create, play soccer, and serve others through your creative and therapeutic works.
Charlie Shahnaian: From the early days of NYC in the "Blimp Room" to sitting next to you on a flight to Los Angeles during one chapter of your life only to see how future chapters unfolded with grace and restoration. It has truly been wonderful knowing you for so many years and watching you grow into the man, husband, father, and artist you are today. Plus, you are one of the kindest and funniest people I know. Keep writing!
Brian Smith: My futurist, poetic friend. Thank you for sharing your story, insights, wisdom and ideas with me. I have always appreciated our inspiring and edifying conversations. Blessings on you and your family.

GSS: My friend, brother and colleague. I've learned so much from you: how you show up in the world, under the radar, with exquisite taste, spirituality, and the unique ability to support special individuals and storytellers. I am grateful you are in my life.

Denise Spatafora: My fellow Italian and New Yorker, you unlocked something inside of me a long time ago that has helped me define and design life on my terms. Your passion, heart, and intelligence inspire. You are one of the people who has always brought out the best in me.

CJ Stanford: Thank you for being such a good friend and neighbor, you to me and your family to ours. You're an amazing husband and dad, and we are blessed to have you, Courtney, and your children in our lives and to share the same affinities for faith, reading, family (and coffee. I know this next chapter of life will be hard but beautiful.

Manie Stein: Of all people to appreciate a nautical journey, it is you. To see you literally come off the sea to begin a new adventure . . . to find your land legs with your lovely wife, Laura, and to befriend your humble, gentlemanly soul. I am blessed we were not ships passing in the night, but that we met and have you in our landlocked lives.

John Sullivan: You plucked me out of a hallway at NYU and asked me to audition for your first feature film. This proved to be the most rewarding experience of my short-lived film acting career. You introduced me to Jeff Buckley, and that collaboration and moment in time were truly special: when things were made independently on Steenbecks, dreams, and fumes. That was a golden time in my early years in NYC. I learned a lot from you. Thanks, ya stutterin' . . .

Tyler Thigpen: If anybody understands the unique journey and grand adventures of life, it is you. Your perspective, soul, and brain are invested in helping to pave unchartered paths for young new heroes, stories, and journeys. Despite the storms you've faced, the horizon is bright and the spheres you lead in are better because you're in them. Your passion, heart, and intellect inspire. Much love.

Rick Toscano: You are one of the biggest truth seekers I know. Your courage, critical thinking, and creativity have always inspired me. It's been a long time since we connected, but I wanted you to know that I respect you. I'm grateful for all you stand for. Keep being you, Rick!

Micheal Thompson: From next door neighbor discussing books to good friend. To see what you have built and where you came from is a miracle and inspiration. I have loved our many discussions about dreaming, placemaking, and serving. Not to mention, hooping. I hope we can find something to build together soon. Stay true to who you are and to your values because where you are going is so far away from where you came from. The best is yet to come for your family. Blessings, brother!

Jenny Torres: Have we had some conversations or what? From parenting to soccer to basketball. You are one of the cool, true souls. So happy you're in my life. Thanks for taking care of my big head!

Stan Tucker: My friend, thank you for your passion for literacy and reading, a passion that is infectious and effective. I look forward to reading the chapters of your family's life and legacy as they are written.

Jason Umidi: Who would have ever thought helping a complete stranger arrange flowers for his wife would lead to a lifelong friendship? Your story, life and testimony are inspiring, an ongoing portrait of redemption and restoration. It's a blessing to call you a friend and walk through life on the road of grace and mercy together. I look forward to what is next.

Jonas Wadler: To think our friendship originated with me thinking you were trying to break into my West Village apartment at 3:00 a.m. From the trenches of Restaurant Nam to Los Angeles and Atlanta, we have enjoyed many memories, conversations, and laughs. You are a pure heart, sweet soul, and brother to everyone who knows you.

Danny Wildman: My honest, vulnerable, and tenacious friend. You and Anna are some of the best gifts from New York City and Los Angeles (not to mention the gift of introducing Denise to me). Your entrepreneurial spirit and commitment to family, faith and friendship continue to inspire. What you have overcome so you can help others do the same is amazing.

Todd Wilkerson: I think the world of you. You are such a good friend to everyone, a true talent as an actor, comedian, and illustrator. Your gifts as a husband and girl dad are amazing too. You have unwavering faith and are loyal, hilarious, and authentic. Keep drawing & creating! Go Knicks!

Scott Teems: From the days of The Haven, to making our wedding video to your Georgia-born storytelling passion being shared with the world, it has been a blessing to see your marriage, children, and career blossom.

Kevin Higgins and **Jason Shurte:** You both are the best I brought away from that chapter of being "Chief" in the trenches with you. Our connective tissue is strongly built on memories, June birthdays and our love for food and one another. I look forward to a reunion.

Rob Forster: What a genuine heart, sweet soul and wonderful Dad. So kind, gentle and intentional. From Irving Blvd. to the Deep South, you took a risk to build something unique and inspiring. Keep running and dreaming my friend. I am happy you are in my life.

Christian Westhof: As a fellow girl dad and husband to another October 26 wife, I have always respected your intellect, witty humor, and unpretentious heart. You've been through a lot on your journey to Ithaka and have handled it with grace, patience, and compassion.

Nick Yoda: Solvitur ambulando. From the early days of high school until your current midlife crisis, you have evolved into a unique individual–with battle wounds, ink, and travels to prove it. You have molded yourself with passion and reckless abandon like the candles you pour. You are a loyal and intellectually curious soul. I am grateful for the decades of friendship. Blessings on the next leg of the journey.

Neighbors: Mimi Tin, Melanie & Mike Duncan, Nita Tin, Jody Noland, Sandra & Dan McFarland, Taylor & Daniel Bashta, Molly & Ed Worrell, Nadria & Omar Lyn, Betsy Rapier, Sineat & Joe Heintzelman, Shannon & Clayton Wagar, Marion & Butch Harrison, Courtney & CJ Stanford, Laura O'Neill, Ashley Edwards, Carol & Jeff Barbee, Emily & David Zamora, Laura & Scott Patak, Mackenzie & Alston Causey, Mikki & David Lewis, Cindy & Joe Castillo, Emily & Joe Hanna, Hannah & Taber Cheo, Meg & Pat Barrett, Mela & Matt Geipel, , Callie & Jason Burkey, Nancy & Mike Meyer, Will James, Meg & Kyle Reichenbach, Lisa & Jordan Brunson, Tela & Josh Kane, Terri & Mike Younker, Gail & Bob Werstlein, Carmen & Aaron Coe, Michelle & Mike Hazelton, Shelly Brown, and Stephen Brown. Each of you are a blessing to our family.

Bill Lynch: My friend, we would not be here without you. Thank you for your vision and friendship. I look forward to what you build next!

Topaz Adizes: Although it has been a very long time, your graceful and creative soul left a long-lasting impression on mine. You are cut from a different cloth, one that should be wrapped around all artists for inspiration and a stronger sense of humanity and connection. I hope we can collaborate on something one day. Much love to you!

Rachel McDonald: I love your soulful, Southern, gritty storytelling sensibilities. I am so grateful we met and had the opportunity to make something together. Our families have now become our best stories. I hope we can collaborate again! We send you much love from the south!

Steve Trayner: My ginger brother from another mother. A kindred spirit, intellectually curious and poetic heart; how you navigate life, and literally the world, while being a great Girl Dad and husband. You can't do it without strong faith, strong community and strong coffee!

Gale Harold: A Georgia-born Renaissance man. You are an original. Your artistry and athleticism, your love for theatre, film, and storytelling, your wit, offbeat humor and your ability to get trapped in elevators in the middle of the night . . . all of it inspires. I hope we can work together again. Or, at least, drink coffee together on Georgia red clay.

Josh Pence: You are one of the most gentle-hearted humans I know. The way your show up in the world with artistry, kindness, and empathy is a gift to everyone. I am blessed to know you and hope to see you soon. Jonathan Graham: It has been great getting to know you, your family and your hearts for storytellers. Thank you for all you do to serve a community of artists. We are happy you, Carly and your boys are here.

The Element Team: Joubin Bral, Edgar Estrada, Noel Peterson, and Russell Paulson, you are a big part of my life journey. Thank you for the opportunity to work alongside such a motley crew through ups and downs, marriages (engagements, RJP!), children and business. It has never been dull and always an adventure. Take care now, Pete.

The Funky Shack: Dawn and Jennifer, what you built through dreaming, determination and grit is inspiring and a life-source to our community. You create momentary art through flowers and provide a beautiful space to support young entrepreneurs and creatives!

Woodstone Bakery: Shellane and Daniel, thank you for being a beloved staple in our community. Some of this book was written in Woodstone, where community and coffee art are made daily.

Scholar & Scribe: Carmen, Shelly and Tela, your bookstore opening embodies the enduring spirit of literature, poetry, and story. Thank you for speaking the love language of creatives and opening something that makes our hearts sing. And a special, poetic thanks to Rae!

Chef Andrea Montobbio, Carmine Noce, David Gibbs, and The Enzo Team: Your canvas is the kitchen. You create momentary art every day. Thank you for gifting our community with food, a sense of belonging, and the support of local artists.

My Fellow Hoopers: Thank you for challenging me and making me a better player. You help me develop my game, IQ, and continued passion for basketball. It is a true joy to know and play with such an interesting, diverse group of individuals; the OGs, Uncs and Young Bucks alike. You are coaches and friends in your own ways and influence me on and off the court. A very special thanks to those I have hooped with over the years:

Ace Marrero, Aiden Lawrence, Adam Glendye, Alex Dunn, AJ Doyley, Andrew Doyley, Asad Majeed, Austin McGuffie (all the McGuffie brothers, and Camden, a rising basketball star), Brandon Tyloch, Bruce, Caleb Latimer, Carlos DeJesus, Charlie Kersten, Chris Daniel, CJ Smith, Brayden Meeks, Colin Bugbee, Corey Warren, Cristan Dawson, Damiani Matta, Daylen Dawson, Daelen Smalls, Darius Beresford, Davin Thomas-Dallas, Denmark "Deyo" Yongco, Derrick Beresford, Devin Smalls, DJ, "Step-Back-Three" Drake Geipel, Dom Kegel, Eddie Robinson, Everett Lawrence, Ezra Coe, Farrukh Bhojwani, Gabriel Martin, Graham Reichenbach, Grey Chitwood, Hayden Long, Indy North, Isiah Gregory, Jack Louneoubonh, Jacob Lee, Jaden Warner, Jason Jackson, Jamal Cook, Jamie Waltermire, Jaden "Rocket" Carr, Jake Kennon, James Carr, Jaylen Romero, Javeir Comrie, Jelani Chapman, Jesse Lindsley, Jikeme Daniels, Joe Smith, Joey Cheriscat, Jordon McKinney, Josiah Smith, Julian Hoskins, Justin Perez, Keaton Hargrove, Keenan Reed, Lawrence Parker, Lawrence Smith, Joey Tleiji, "Cool-Hand" Luke Cagle, Matt Douglas, Matt Geipel, Max Latimer, Micah Delesline, Micah Silva, Micheal Thompson, Mike Edwards, Neftali, Mike Graham, Big Nial, Nick Plummer, Nikolas Davis, Numair Sohani, Oliver Langham, Omari Hemmings, Oswin Thigpen, Parker Stanford, Parthasarathy Chintala, Phil Dang, Preston Dang, Rashad Hodge, Reese Edwards, Ronald Hall, Ryan Robinson, Saleem Reed (my favorite 1v1 opponent), Samuel Wakefield III, Sean Beresford, Sundiata Salaam-Bey, Tray Meeks, Tre "Kyrie" Hightower, Trey Hill, Tyler Kaleb, Tyler Mullner, Tyler Thigpen, Wesley Robinson, Xavier Moore, The Hoopers at Kedron whose names I don't know, The Forest School Phoenixes, and Sara Coliano at The Atlanta Hawks.

I love you guys! And I can't wait to sink a **three** on you soon!

Thanks to my professional inspirations: Larry Bird, Jason Williams, Kyrie Irving, Luka Dončić, Michael Jordan, Stephen Curry, Kevin Durant, John Stockton, Kobe Bryant, Trae Young, Bill Russell, LeBron James, Jayson Tatum, Pete Maravich, Anthony Edwards, and Jaylen Brown (Marietta boy!).

And finally:

To All the Dreamers and Doers:

This is a love letter to you.

Keep dreaming, daring and doing.

The amount of time we have on this planet is a gift.

It is also a vapor.

Make it count.

Give your all.

Do what makes your heart sing.

Love others.

Take care of your soul.

The journey is challenging,

but it can be beautiful.

If you are not there yet,

you are here . . .

. . . exactly where you are supposed to be.

Surround yourself with the *dreamers* and the *doers*,
the *believers* and the *thinkers,*
but most of all,
surround yourself with *those*
who see the greatness within you,
even when you don't see it yourself.
—Edmund Lee

MICHAEL ALBANESE

A NATIVE OF NEW YORK CITY, MICHAEL GREW UP IN MARIETTA, GEORGIA.
HE LOVES COFFEE, BASKETBALL, AND ALL EXPRESSIONS OF ART.
MICHAEL LIVES AND DREAMS IN ATLANTA WITH HIS WIFE, ACTRESS WYNN EVERETT,
AND THEIR TWO DAUGHTERS (AND TWO CATS).

HE HAS NOT YET ARRIVED.

JJ RICHARDS

BORN IN BUENOS AIRES AND NOW LIVING AND WORKING IN MADRID FOR
THE PAST SEVENTEEN YEARS, JJ RICHARDS IS A MULTIDISCIPLINARY ARTIST,
DESIGNER, PRACTICING ART THERAPIST, AND AUTHOR.

JJ RUNS WORKSHOPS AND MENTORING PROGRAMS FOCUSING ON THE PROCESS OF
CREATION. SHE COMPLETED HER ART STUDIES AT THE ART STUDENTS LEAGUE OF
NEW YORK, THE CONTEMPORARY ART ACADEMY OF LONDON, AND AT
THE ESCUELA ARGENTINA DE ARTETERAPIA IN BUENOS AIRES.

JJ IS AN ACTIVE MEMBER OF THE CENTER OF APPLIED JUNGIAN STUDIES IN
CAPE TOWN AND IS CURRENTLY FURTHERING HER STUDIES IN ART HISTORY AT
THE ART EXPLORA ACADEMY BY THE PARIS-SORBONNE UNIVERSITY.

SHE HAS NOT YET ARRIVED EITHER.

"Momentary Art" with Georgia
at Woodstone Bakery

Tune my heart to sing Thy grace.

IN LOVING MEMORY:

MY FATHER, SALVATORE JAMES ALBANESE

RENATA WALZ
LARRY CARPENTER
ADAM EPSTEIN
DAVID HANDELMAN
LINDA JONES
RICHARD CLARK
BLANCA VIRULA

Made in United States
Troutdale, OR
10/08/2024

23546126R00126